Sounding:

Ultimate Control

BarbarianSpy

FOR LITERARY HEAT

www.BarbarianSpy.com

WARNING: This book is for sale to **ADULT AUDIENCES ONLY**. Contains graphic gay male sex, BDSM elements, domination, bondage, reluctance, multiple partners, anal sex, nongraphic violence, and gay love all of which may be considered offensive by some readers.

All sexually active characters in this work are at least 18 years of age.

Published by BarbarianSpy
Jindalee St
Toronto, NSW 2283
AUSTRALIA

Sounding:

Ultimate Control

habu

Table of Contents

Introduction

Sounding: Ultimate Control provides, in paperback, six stories by habu of what possibly is the most intimate and dominating sex act one man can perform on another, one that is so intimate and extreme that it is only rarely written about. The wanding of another man's urethral canal is a fetish of domination, trust, and control. One slip of the wand and a man can be ruined. Few engage in the activity, but those who do know that it can provide the ultimate arousal and sexual satisfaction.

The first work in this anthology is an expanded version of "Dark Angel Sounding," appearing here in paperback form for the first time ever. Probably habu's most controversial and popular previously published work—"Dark Angel Sounding" certainly has generated more discussion than has anything he has published before. The story follows in intimate and detailed description, the deepening subjugation of a young man to the ultimate control of an older man—his Dark Angel.

"Career Guidance" is the story of a young-looking Hollywood star who has rebelled against always playing young, boyish roles by engaging in a life of debauchery, including publicly gossiped-about encounters in a car with a transvestite. His agent, as a last-chance measure, uses the controlling mechanism of sounding to put the young actor in his place and attempt to save his career as well as fulfill the long-frustrated sexual fantasies of the agent himself.

In "Searching for It" a young sailor from Vancouver, who is on the East Coast of the United States for the first time in his life, working on a private yacht, goes searching for sexual relief in the gay district of New York near the docks area at the foot of Manhattan. He finds something he's never experienced before, the tease of a sounding-like technique, in a gay club and winds up kidnapped to be given the full sounding experience himself.

A high-paid male prostitute is given a "punishment" assignment by his pimp to provide unusual and taxing services to a kinky doctor in "Prepped and Sounded." And "Roswell's Frontier Motel" brings an alien variation of sounding into the supernatural world for a highly unusual take on this form of male sex act.

The concluding story, "Do You Trust Me?," takes the reader to the picturesque Italian harbor town of Positano, where a young fisherman and café singer shows that he's willing to do anything to leave Italy and break into movies—even a very specific kind of movie.

This page has been deliberately left blank.

Dark Angel Sounding

Prologue

I was so young and wanting to experience sensations to the fullest—and unknowing in what I wanted—when my Dark Angel found me and seduced me. But he knew what I wanted. He knew I wanted to be dominated and fully possessed. I did not know in my wildest dreams how deeply and fully I could be controlled and dominated and possessed. But my Dark Angel knew. He knew of the most possessing and invasive—and taboo—of all fetishes in the taking and domination of a man by another man.

Chapter 1: Sounding

My angel was taking me to the darker side, introducing me to new sensations and passions, higher levels of arousal than I had ever known before in my heretofore vanilla sex life. He was an addiction, a dangerous habit to feed, I fully realized, and I had come back to his den willingly, wanting to know what more there was, what new heights my passion could reach. My head kept saying no or at least to go slow, but my body yearned for his touch, for his domination, for reaching new heights of body awareness and pleasure under his guidance.

I had returned voluntarily to his basement room, as he knew I would. My hands were handcuffed to the brass headboard welded to the wall, and I was kneeling, facing the wall, on a stained mattress.

We were beyond the spankings and light lashings that had made my tender ass, inner thighs, and cock and balls red swollen and ultrasensitive to the touch. We were even beyond the soothing and arousing attention his lips and tongue had paid to my swollen thighs, tender kissings that had crescendoed to bitings that had me screaming for mercy and then to the rimming and invasion of my ass channel with his searching tongue with its tantalizing knobbed stud.

We were now on to a new phase. He knelt between my thighs, very close into me, the studs of the leather harness criss-crossing his bulging chest rubbing against my shoulder blades, his rock-hard cock, with its Prince Albert pierced head ring rubbing between my swollen thighs. He had one hand firmly palmed on my lower belly, holding me into his pelvis, and he held a purple silicone ribbed and nubbed dildo in his other hand, pressing it between my lips. I took it in as I would have willingly taken in his cock—as I, indeed, already had taken in his cock before I'd been handcuffed to the wall—and I made love to it as I knew he wanted me to, taking in its measure, knowing that it soon would be working its thick eight inches or more into my puckered hole.

The Dark Angel was humming. He had done this before when he was engrossed in what he was doing and when, it seemed, he was being especially aroused by the activity. I had learned in our earlier sessions that this marked his being in a zone of his own while he worked my body and that as long as he was humming, it made no difference what I might feel or want—he was going to pursue what he felt like doing and what he wanted.

He pulled the moistened dildo from between my lips and sat back on his haunches briefly, lathering the tool up with lube, all the time telling me how nice my body was and how he was going to play me like a violin. No, he said, not like a violin. That was too refined. He was going to work me like a factory machine, roughly and strongly, one that worked with a punching rod, pistoning the rod inside it endlessly and forcefully. I moaned at the image he was providing and longed for him to cover me once again, to hold me close and dominate me.

And then he *was* covering me again, and I felt the bulbous-capped end of the silicone dildo against my throbbing asshole. He told me not to hold back in voicing my responses, which he hardly needed to have done, because I lurched and arched my back and cried out my mixed pain and ecstasy from the moment the slick dildo entered me, until it had screwed all the way in to the hilt. I screamed out, protesting at the stretching and rubbing and rough digging it was doing as I felt each ripple and nub working the walls of my canal. Doing so made him laugh.

All the time he was telling me how the dildo was nothing compared to the take-no-prisoners invader his own cock would be, and he soon was proving that. He made me stand up on the mattress, my legs spread wide, and my torso slanted down to where my hands were cuffed to the wall, and exchanged the swirling rotation of the dildo for his own thicker and longer cock. I groaned and grunted and screamed out again in both fear and welcome as his heavily veined cock, with that ring in the tip—thinly sheathed with a condom that didn't interfere with the sensations provided by stroking of the ring and rippling of the veins as he plowed up into me—worked inside my gut.

When I felt the studs of the cock ring at the root of his shaft attack the rim of my hole, he covered my nipples with both his hands and started to worry them with his pinching fingers and nails. Then he leaned his lips up to my ear and asked me if I was ready for the piston machine to be turned on.

I moaned back my desire for him to take me long and hard and furiously, and then I cried out once more as he bit my ear lobe and continued chewing lightly on that as he began to pump me hard, in long strokes, punishing my ass walls with that twirling cock ring of his.

My knees gave up to the onslaught of his vigorous fucking, and I collapsed onto the mattress, the Dark Angel coming down with me without losing purchase on my hole. He covered me close from on top and kept pistoning his rod into me. I was pushing my ass back at him with each stroke, which caused my engorged dick to slide across the mattress, and at length I added my own cum stain to the mattress to join that of so many who he boastfully told me had preceded me there.

With a lurch and a cry of victory, the Dark Angel also spent himself within me, and we lay there panting and sighing until we had regained a regular pattern of breathing.

While he was uncuffing me and leading me off to the shower, he said, "Dress after we've showered and then I want to take you somewhere."

I was mildly disappointed, because in our previous session, it had been after we had showered that he had really shown me what I had been missing for so long in arousal and a fantastic fuck. But he was the boss, and I was the slave in our relationship.

After we showered, he fed me, telling me that I'd want to build up all the strength I could for his surprise, and then we were on his motorcycle and moving into an even more "iffy" part of the city than where his digs were located.

He pulled up in a warehouse district and we entered a nondescript door in a blank wall and followed the stairs to the basement. We were in a low-ceilinged, smoke-filled room that was teeming with men in various stages of undress, arousal, and release activity. There were bars set up on three sides and small tables, with chairs, most occupied, not all by a single person, all circling around a center platform, with a spotlight shining down.

Two men were performing on the platform. There was a wedge-like cushion in the center of the platform, with arm and leg restraints at each corner. A youngish, lithe, red-headed guy, with a flowing mane of hair, was reclining on the wedge, ass tilted up on the higher end of the slant, and torso draped back toward the lower end, with head propped up on a slightly elevated end. His arms were bent up, and his wrists were cuffed in the restraints on the sides of the wedge beside his head. His torso was stretched out fully to show off his fine musculature. His ankles were cuffed at the sides of the other end of the wedge, although there were lines attached to the wedge that permitted the wide spreading of the young man's legs. A burlier, muscle-bound, completely hairless man, wearing a headsman-style mask that covered the top of his head and came down to below his eyes was hovering between the young man's legs. I could tell the young man was both beleaguered and enjoying himself by the screaming he was doing—much of it in the form of asking for more attention and testing than he was getting.

I had no more gathered the impression that the burly man was covered with jewelry piercings and that the trussed youth had one of the longest dongs I'd ever seen, however, before the Dark Angel pulled me over to one of the bars, perched on a barstool, and pulled my ass into his pelvis between his spread and possessing legs. He encased me in his arms and rested his chin on my shoulder.

He had ordered beers while he was folding my body into his, and while we waited for them to arrive, my eyes adjusted to the dimly lit room, undulating with men in heat and full rut, many of their eyes riveted on the stage. As the Dark Angel worked his hand under the waistband of my trousers and cupped my balls and played with my cock, my attention went back to the stage, where I saw the young man straining his muscles, his head thrown back, emitting loud moans from a slack, stretched mouth.

And then I saw why, and I involuntarily tensed inside the Dark Angel's embrace. The burly dominator was kneeling at the end of the high side of the wedge, between the receiver's wide-spread, cuffed legs. He was holding the end of a silver, curved, rather thin wand between two of his fingers. And he was slowly pushing it into the piss slit of the young man. As it slid in farther, the young man was panting hard and crying out a series of "yeses," which was the only indication I had that he was enjoying this invasion of the most intimate area of his body. The burly man twirled the wand slightly inside the slit, and the young man groaned and grunted his ecstasy.

17

And then the wand was being extracted—slowly and dramatically. A sigh went through the audience. When extracted, it looked like a good four inches had been inside the slit.

I felt like I couldn't breathe and discovered that this was largely because the Dark Angel was holding me tight, almost smothering me in his embrace. And he was humming softly to himself.

I wiggled and his embrace slackened, but it tightened up again as we both watched the burly man take a thicker and slightly longer wand from a case and slowly insert that inside the slit in the younger man's cock, now harder and even longer than before. The younger man strained at his cuffs and screamed to the ceiling, but he was making every attempt to hold very still in the knowledge of how precise the insertions had to be. Once more a slide in and a swirl and the wave of a heavy sigh across the audience. And then the long slide out. The third wand was even thicker. The youth's piss slit was being stretched open to where I could see, even from the distance that I was standing, that the hole was gaping.

I closed my eyes tight as this third wand disappeared inside the young man's penis. I couldn't watch this; I didn't even want to think of this. My own penis was feeling the pain and tension in sympathy—or so I thought until I realized that the Dark Angel had a finger at my piss slit and was trying to force the finger into me.

I tensed once more and the Dark Angel whispered in my ear, "So what do you think?"

"What do I think?" I whispered back, dumbfounded. "What do I think of what's happening up there?"

"It's called sounding," the Dark Angel murmured. "I take it you aren't impressed."

"Impressed is not the word for it," I said with a moan, which told him all he needed to know about what I thought about it.

He changed tactics, "I meant, though, what do you think of the restraint wedge. Does that look like fun?"

"Yes, yes, it does," I admitted, opening my eyes again to take another look at the wedge, and seeing the fourth, thicker wand being inserted.

While this wand was going in, the young man, who had remained relatively calm for the third wand, cried out again, declaring that he was about to cum—to get the wand out. And the burly man responded to this urging and slid the wand out just ahead of a prodigious spurting of semen onto the burly man's belly. Amid scattered applause in the audience, the burly man laughed, licked off the young man's penis, and started forcing a pinkie finger into the now greatly enlarged piss slit. The young man was moaning and writhing again.

"Well, that's why we're really here," the Dark Angel returned to our conversation. "I've rented a cell here for this afternoon. It features one of those wedges."

He stopped in mid thought, however, the attention of both of us going to the stage now. The young man was being uncuffed, the wedge was pushed off the stage, and it was replaced with a thicker rectangle. Some sort of pillowy-padded platform with cuffs at the four corners again. The young red head went down on this on his belly and his wrists were cuffed at the upper corners. His legs were bent up on the sides of the platform, with his upper thighs strapped at the sides and the ankles cuffed in close to the bottom corners. This arrangement presented his ass to the bottom edge of the platform, and his long dong hanging down the bottom edge. The burly man was kneeling at the young man's ass and was tonguing his hole and stroking down on his cock.

"As I was saying," the Dark Angel went on, "are you interested in trying a wedge?"

"Yes."

"Now?"

"Yes."

As we worked our way through the crowd to a door at the other side of the room, the burly man was working his cock into the ass of the young red head. He had one palm pushing down on the small of the young man's back and had the other fist buried in the young man's flowing main, pulling his head back, so everyone could see the fucking-induced contortions of his face and clearly hear his cries as the burly man's cock plowed into him.

I was all atremble when we reached the small cell. Only a centered platform supporting another one of those wedges occupied the room. The Dark Angel slowly undressed and cuffed me, facing up, on the wedge. The wedge was extremely comfortable and sensual, yielding to ever contour of my body. Then as I watched, he undressed himself. He looked good and evil at the same time, and my cock started to emit precum at the mere sight of that thick dong with the Prince Albert cock ring in its head.

Then he did the unexpected. He blindfolded me.

I objected, but he said he wanted me to experience everything this time from just the sensation of touch. He crouched over me and kissed me on the lips. Then he kissed me on each nipple in turn—right before he attached clamps to my nipples. This was an entirely new, not fully pleasant experience, for me, and I whimpered a bit. But he paid no attention to me; he was humming. I could tell that I was going to be entirely at his mercy. And this is what I had wanted. I was addicted. I wanted to experience the edges of arousal and sexual stimulation. As I relaxed and he thumbed the nipple clamps, I began to enjoy what they were doing to my sense of touch.

He tongued and bit my inner thighs for several moments, working his way to my asshole. When he thought me prepared, he started fucking me. He rode me bareback, and the sensation of his veined and ringed cock sliding across my ass canal walls had me moaning and groaning in appreciation. He dug his fingernails into my thighs, and every once in a while he lifted a hand to tweak the nipple clamps. He also hit my hard pecs with a closed fist and slapped my flat belly with an open palm. Giving me a full range of sensations.

The wedge was wonderful. It opened and imprisoned me fully to the Dark Angel's onslaught. The domination was total. But not really total yet. He had more planned.

Before he jacked off, he pulled out of me and I felt his thick, hard cock being slapped against my thighs and then my belly and then on my chest. He took my lips in his and punished my tongue with his tongue stud. Then he knelt on my chest, between my upraised, imprisoned arms, and slapped that dong of his on my face. He forced his cock between my lips, and I deep throated him to his ejaculation, gagging a bit as I swallowed his repeated spurts of semen.

Then he was off of me, and there was a foreboding silence. Then the humming started again. I hadn't been aware of when he'd stopped the humming while he was fucking me, but he must have—because the humming unmistakably was back and in full force.

I felt a hand on my cock, cupping my cock at the root, on the underside—holding my cock up at a raised angle, my hips already being raised by the wedge. Then I turned stone cold and a chill went through my body as I felt the cold steel tip of the wand at my piss slit. I screamed out as the first of the wands slowly entered me there. Violation, stuffing, remarkably little pain, an electric zing through my body, my cock engorging, an indescribable feeling of sensual pleasure—enhanced by the mere thought of now having had every orifice of my body dominated and fucked by my Dark Angel.

"Relax, relax," I was hearing in a soft, soothing, hummed tone. "Relax and go with the feeling. It will be so much better,"

A sucking, emptying feeling as the wand slid out. A strange sense of loss and emptiness when it is gone.

Then a thicker wand, entering me, making me scream again despite myself. Tightening up, but then remembering, and relaxing. But as this wand glided up through my urethra, I knew I was about to cum. I yelled out to the Dark Angel. Asking for mercy. Letting him know I was going to blow. And the wand glided back out and I did blow my wad.

A husky laugh from the Dark Angel and a cleaning of my penis with his tongue. That's it then, I think. Yet another, deeper, darker experience. That was OK then. But then an even thicker wand at my piss slit. Pushing in, stretching me. Loud humming. I cry out. "Oh, God, oh God. Noooo. Yessss. M-o-o-a-n-n . . ."

Chapter 2: The Cube

The phone rang and I sat there and looked at it through five rings. I recognized the number on the caller ID. I wouldn't answer it. After seven rings it would kick over to the machine. Ring number six.

"Hello."

"You know who this is. Come to me."

"Look, I'm sorry, but—"

"Come to me now. Shower and clean yourself out. Don't bother to wear much."

Click.

I sat there, staring at the phone. I wouldn't go. And when I hadn't shown up, that would be the end of it. No more control. No more domination. Finished.

Forty-five minutes later I was ringing his doorbell at the run-down bungalow in a bad part of town. My Dark Angel opened the door and pulled me across the threshold. He started stripping off my clothes as he herded me down the narrow stairs to the basement—to his special basement room.

"I just came to tell you—"

"Skip it. We both know why you came to me. Come over here. Strip down first. All the way down."

"I . . . I. What's that?" I had stripped as he demanded.

"This here? This is a cock ring and ball stretcher. That over there? That's the cube."

He took my cock in his hand and snapped the metal ring around its root, and then he pushed my balls down from my body, as I gave a little surprised lurch, and snapped a wide leather band around where the ball sack came up at the root of my cock, pushing my balls painfully into two tight, egg-sized lumps well below my cock. "Ow, that hurts," I objected nonsensically. "I'm not going to—"

He gave the ball sack a few slaps with the undersides of his closed fingers, and I nearly doubled over in pain. A long, low moan escaped my lips.

"Listen, if you're going to talk through this, I'm going to gag you. Neither of us is going to want that. You're going to want to scream, and I'm going to want to listen to you scream. I'm going to get a certain level of satisfaction out of this, and if it isn't in the screaming, it's going to have to be in something else. Understand?"

Yes, I did think I understood—all too well. I looked longingly at the now closed and locked door leading to the staircase. I wanted to leave. I desperately wanted to not be here. But I was kidding myself. I knew I had been waiting by the phone, waiting for this call. I knew why I was here. I knew I wanted to be here.

"Now this cube over here," he said. "This is your home away from home for today. I'm going to fuck you every way from Sunday on this cube. This cube is going to be your best friend."

My eyes focused on my Dark Angel. He was still both the best looking and most evil looking man I'd seen. He was a swarthy, hairy bear of a man, both a hulk and a hunk, a man of the motorcycle gangs and the walk on the wild side. His big, thick cock, with that Prince Albert ring through the head swung low between his heavily muscled legs. I hyperventilated at the thought of that buried in my ass again and, at the same time, I couldn't wait for it. I was precuming just at the thought of that PA ring dragging along my ass canal walls.

I just followed along dumbly, or rather hobbled, being bothered by the unfamiliar and painful sheathing of my cock and my now-sore balls, over to the cube and stared blankly at it. My Dark Angel was patting the top of it to show me that it was cushy and had some bounce to it. It had a blue cover and was nearly two feet high and a foot and a half tall on each side. There were four cuffs, two each on opposite sides, attached by short chains to the sides of the cube, but there were several other places on the sides of the cube where the chains could be attached.

He told me to kneel on the cube, which I did, and he crouched close behind me, one hand holding my ringed cock, already engorging and standing at attention, while he clipped tit clamps on my nipples. I groaned while he did this, as they were still tender from our last session using them. He just laughed, enjoying my discomfort, making clear who was the boss here.

I could feel his monster cock, with its metal ring at the small of my back, and he was kissing my shoulder. I turned my head and he possessed my mouth with his, pushing in his nub-studded tongue and punishing my tongue and the inner linings of my cheeks with that. I lurched and tried to pull away when he put pressure on my distended balls with a fist and pinched at the tit clamps, but he took my tongue in his teeth and held it firmly while his arms grasped me tight, enjoying my writhing. I stopped fighting him and willed my muscles to relax, to show him I had surrendered, trying to block out the pain at my balls, nipples, and tongue.

When he was satisfied that I was fully under control, he relaxed his grasp at the three points and ran his tongue down my back and buried it between my butt cheeks, his hands holding me in the kneeling position on the cube by grasping my hips. He moved on to fingering me with lube and sliding his fingers in and out of my hole until he was satisfied that I had opened to him sufficiently.

I thought he was going to move in and fuck me then, but he moved away from me and instructed me to lay, chest down, on top of the cube and to extend my legs straight out behind me and support weight on my toes. When I was in this position, he cuffed my hands to either side of the cube near the base. I had my legs close together, in a push-up position, but he told me to spread them wider. This was going to be OK, but not for long.

But he quickly let me know that endurance in this position was going to be one of the main points to this session. I felt the slight sting of leather strips zing across my buttocks.

"Feel that?" my Dark Angel was asking. "If you don't keep your legs in this position until I'm finished with you here, you will feel the lash until you're back in position. Understand?"

"Yes," I said through gritted teeth.

"Yes, what?" he said, and I felt a slight sting from the whip again.

"Yes, sir," I said. I must have given him the answer he wanted, because he moved in between my legs then and started rubbing his cock around on my buttocks and along the insides of my thighs and up and down in my crack. My balls were aching

24

from being distended even further now by gravity, and I whimpered a bit.

The Dark Angel had already told me several times that he liked to hear me whimper, and I could hear him beginning to hum.

And then I felt him entering my ass. But, no, even he wasn't this big. He felt me tremble, and then I was relieved of the pressure.

"Want to see?" he asked with a husky little laugh. "Take a look at these. These are what are going up your ass."

I turned my head to see a flexible length of fairly large-sized anal beads, and I shuddered and my knees began to buckle as he returned to pushing them into my ass. When they were all in, he slowly began to pull them out again, and I heard and felt the popping sound as each plopped back out of my ass. Then they were pushed in again and this time they were jerked out in one motion that had my knees buckling and heading toward the floor.

But the Dark Angel didn't allow them to reach the floor; he got an arm under my thighs and pulled them back up while he switched my butt and the back of my thighs and my back with the stinging leather whip until I had regained my position.

He did move back in between my legs then and entered me with his throbbing cock and stroked me until I was weak in the legs again. When he felt he had me opened up real well, he swung his legs over mine, one at a time, while still plowing me with his cock, and held my legs close together, constricting my hole tightly around his rod.

When I thought I couldn't hold my legs in position any longer and he could feel me cramping up, he pulled out of me and told me I could kneel. He untied the hand cuffs at the front edge of the cube, but he left the cuffs on my wrists. He then sat down on the cube and told me to skewer myself on his cock again, facing away from him. I went back into his lap and started slowly descending my ass on his cock, but he was impatient and took me by the hips and pushed me all the way down until he was fully encased inside me.

He reached down and cuffed my ankles and tied them and my wrist cuffs off on the same attachment at the top back edge of the cube on two sides. So, now I was sitting in his lap, my arms and legs pulled back at each side, hogtied and impaled on his rock-hard cock.

"Now we'll see what full domination is," he said. "You haven't been vocal enough. I want to hear some screaming and begging."

He first pinched the tit clamps on my nipples until I screamed for him to give me mercy on that. He then turned his attention to my tender, distended balls. He squeezed my tight nuts until I screamed in pain and my eyes watered. And then he let loose and told me to turn my head and kiss him. I did, after which he squeezed my balls tight once more, causing me to open my mouth wide in a scream that was stanched by his greedy, tongue-filled kiss. This time he didn't let loose until I was writhing against his chest, and my ass was rotating wildly around on his cock, trying to pull my balls away from his punishing fist.

He finally released me and whispered in my ear, "Remember that. I am now going to possess you as you never have been possessed before. And you are going to love it. And you are going to come back whenever I call you to me. Do you understand?"

"Yes," I whimpered, not understanding really, but ready to agree to anything now. "I'm going to be possessing you in every orifice, and you are calmly going to respond to me. And if you don't, we can always return to tit and ball play. Understand?"

"Yes."

"Yes, what?"

"Yes, sir."

Out came the graduated sounding wands. I shuddered in remembrance, as he selected a thinnish one, cupped my cock in one hand, and slowly inserted the wand six inches up my piss slit with the other. I was panting, avoiding looking at the metal rod being run into my piss slit, but trying to move as little as possible and doing everything I could not to scream in fear of what he might decide to do during this delicate maneuver. I felt filled and clogged far up my urethra. He slowly rotated the wand inside me, and I wanted to tear away from my bounds and escape, but that wasn't going to happen.

He slowly pulled the wand out and went to a larger size. I took my breath in and stifled a scream of violation and invasion as

26

it entered me and teased the piss canal to widen to his attention. But, instead, I leaned back into his chest and tried to relax as the thicker wand moved deeper toward the bladder than the first one had. This time after it had traveled some distance, my canal grabbed it and pulled it inside and the Dark Angel had to grip the end of the wand to keep from losing it inside me.

The tension was heavy and I began to sweat.

"Worried, aren't you?" he whispered in my ear. "I could so easily ruin you for life right now, couldn't I?"

"Yes," I whimpered.

To add to the fear, he started his hips in an up-and-down movement on the cube, moving his cock inside me. What he was doing must have been a great turn on for him, because his cock kept growing and thickening inside me, and he was humming again, more loudly this time. I was terrified that the movement of his hips and cock would cause him to lose a solid grip on the wand, and I started to moan.

He laughed and, while continuing the rocking motion of his cock, slowly pulled the wand out. The next one was a couple of sizes larger, and I was moaning at just the sight of it. It was no more than half way in when I felt my balls tighten and I screamed that I was about to cum. He pulled the wand out to permit me to shoot off onto the floor beyond the cube and then he slowly reinserted it. When it was in a good six inches, he took the hand that had been cupping my cock away and inserted his thumb in my mouth. I automatically began sucking on his thumb, knowing this was what he wanted. Then he had his three middle fingers in my mouth, being sucked like they were a cock.

"There, full possession," he crooned to me. "Servicing every one of your orifices at once. Fucking all three orifices at once. Isn't that nice? I said, isn't that nice?"

He pulled his fingers out of my mouth long enough for me to whisper a "Yes," and then another "yes" to his question that wasn't this what I had come back to him for—and would continue coming back to him for.

He released me from all of my bondage then, but immediately hauled me over on the floor beside the cube; wrapped a plow belt around my belly; crouched behind me, pulling my pelvis up to his; and fucked me vigorously doggie style until he had shot off deep inside me.

When he unlocked the door to the basement room and let me escape, he said, "You will come again when I call. You belong to me." And I did not contradict him.

Chapter 3: Gang's All Here

The call had come in the late afternoon, and I stood shivering on the small porch of the run-down little bungalow, even though the sun was still burning hotly. The Dark Angel opened the door, and, when I started for the stairs to the basement on my own, he grabbed me by the arm and pushed me toward the back of the house instead.

We entered what must have been his bedroom. The first thing I saw was the large wire dog's cage in the corner and a chill went down my spine. I wasn't fond of dogs, and someone like the Dark Angel was sure to have a large, mean brute of one. Then I saw the bed. Just a double bed, but then I saw rising up from the sides, near the foot of the bed, what looked like two metal shepherd's hooks. I saw that cuffs on short chains were attached to the top of the hooks and that what looked like a wide band of black leather sling was also attached there and hung down between the hooks.

The Dark Angel wasted no time in getting into the session. He stripped me down and cuffed my hands to the tops of the hooks and made me kneel on the bed, pointed toward the headboard. My chest rested on and was supported by the band of leather. He quickly prepared my ass for his cock, came down onto the bed with his knees, and was soon buried deep inside me and driving my ass walls wild with that Prince Albert cock ring of his. This was what I liked. This was what I came here for—his luscious cock pumping me hard.

Shortly into the fuck, he came off the bed onto his feet and lifted my legs and swung them out, holding them to his hips. I was suspended in air now, my chest straining against the leather sling, and he was pumping my ass hard and deep, swinging me forward and pulling his cock back and then ramming me deep as he pulled my body back toward his.

I was sure he was going to finish me like this; I wanted him to finish me like this. But he suddenly stopped fucking me. I could tell he was close to blowing, but he stopped. He uncuffed me and told me I'd better go take a piss, that maybe it would be a while before I'd be able to do that again. With a great sense of foreboding, I went into the small bathroom off of the bedroom and did my best to evacuate myself.

When I returned, I saw that he was sitting on the end of the bed and had the ball stretcher he had used on me in the last session down in his basement in one hand and the case containing the set of sounding wands in the other. I moaned as soon as I saw them and involuntarily turned toward the bedroom door, wanting to escape. But I knew there was no escape from him.

"Come here," he commanded.

I hesitated.

"I said come here, now," he repeated in a low growl.

I slowly walked over to him and he pulled me to him, spun me around, and sat me in his lap. I cried out in pain, as he forced my ass down hard on his engorged cock. I was once more skewered to his lap. I involuntarily lurched as he got the ball stretcher snapped between the root of my cock and the pulled-tight balls again. This time he cuffed my wrists, my arms spread out wide, on the hook apparatuses at either side of the bed. After he'd bounced me up and down on his cock for a few minutes and punished my ass walls with his ringed cock, he spread his legs wide and then lifted my legs out even wider on top of them and told me to lay back into his chest. When I was a little slow in doing that, he reached down with one hand and squeezed my balls and pinched my nipples with the other hand and told me he was going to continue doing so until I settled down. I fought through the pain and settled as well as I could under the circumstances.

I whimpered as I heard the sounding wand case being unzipped. Out came a wand a size larger than he had last used on me. I lay as still as I could as it slowly entered my piss slit and worked its way deep down my urethra. When it was in a good seven inches, the Dark Angel slowly rotated it about and moved it back and forth, nudging my piss canal to widen. He was humming again now, in his own zone of pleasure. He held the rod there deep inside me for a minute or more and then he turned his face down to me and, as I knew he expected, I met his mouth in a kiss. He was slowly pulling the wand out as he kissed me deeply, possessing my mouth, not permitting me to cry out.

He pulled his mouth away from me and selected the next thicker sounding wand.

"Auggh! Ahhhh," I did cry out now as this one traveled through my piss canal. The wands seemed impossibly thick now. He was humming loudly. I was afraid I was beginning to hyperventilate and was panting with shallow breaths, trying to hold my pelvis perfectly still.

I wanted to pass out and think I almost did as the fourth wand entered me. I collapsed against the Dark Angel's chest, fully spent, every nerve of my body tuned to that thick, thick rod teasing my piss canal to spread wide as it invade deep inside me. I felt I was close to coming, but I was too weak to do anything about it.

And then the Dark Angel pulled the wand out. And he must have felt me close to orgasm, as I could tell from his ragged breathing, was he. When the tip of the wand exited, he squeezed my balls and he and I ejaculated at the same time, me in a profusion of cream just flowing out of my beleaguered piss slit and he deep inside my ass.

I thought the ordeal was over then. He was passionately kissing me, and I thought he had had enough. When he disengaged, I just nodded my head back on his shoulder and stared at the ceiling, wondering what came next—both fearing and aroused by what may come next.

I felt cold steel at my piss slit again, and I jerked my head down in surprise. I was just in time to see the full length of the four-inch swordlike metal rod as the Dark Angel pushed it into the widened piss slit all the way to the hilt. There was a metal ring attached to the hilt by a short chain, and he proceeded to force the head of my cock through this and push it to the rim, where the head met the shaft.

"This is a penis plug," the Dark Angel explained. "You will wear this until I take it out of you. And I wouldn't even think of trying to piss with it in; you would not like the result."

I knew better than to ask him why he was doing this to me. I knew it was all about dominating me—the most intimate form of domination—and me accepting that without question. The longer I took to surrender to him fully to his satisfaction, the more of this I would have to endure.

But this is what I came here for. To be totally dominated. To surrender my all to my Dark Angel.

"And these are weights," he went on to say, showing me tiny black cylinders. "These are going on the ball stretcher to ensure your balls distend nicely."

After attaching these to the stretcher and listening to me moan for a minute at being stretched like this, he told me to kneel down on the floor and grab my ankles with my hands. When I had done so, he cuffed the wrist and ankle together on either side and frog marched me over to the cage. I was whimpering again as he put me in the cage, hunched over on my haunches. I now knew what kind of dog he had; it was me.

He left me there for I don't know how long, as the shadows lengthened and the light in the room dimmed.

At length I heard voices in the front of the house—men's voices—and an increasing number of them. The Dark Angel was having a party.

After a while, he came back into the room, beer in hand, still naked and his cock at full attention, and released me from the cage, the cuffs, the penis plug, and the ball stretcher. He told me I could—and should—take a leak in the bathroom, which I sorely needed to do, and that I should take a quick shower as well. I was all cramped up and could hardly stand, but I shuffled straight for the bathroom and for relief.

When I emerged from the bathroom, the party had been moved to the bedroom. Seven hulking biker types in addition to the Dark Angel, were spread out around the room, waiting for me to appear. They all were naked. And they were all muscle men, except that a few had a bit of a beer belly. They whistled and gave cat calls when they saw me, all apparently half drunk. I was passed around the men for the next three hours.

They all fucked me at least once, and some of them more than once. All of them were rough with me, but some were rougher than others. The Dark Angel just stood back and let me be banged time and time again. Some attached me to the hook apparatus and fucked me either from the rear or missionary style with my legs opened wide and cuffed to the stakes. Once in the latter case, I also had a guy sitting on my chest and feeding his cock into my mouth. A black dude wanted to wrestle, and, at first, wrestled me to a 69 position and then, when I had sucked him big on the Dark Angel's command, wrestled me to where he was covering my back close and pistoning his heavy dick down into me. Another guy had the nifty idea of stuffing me back in the cage and fucking me through the wire sides. He had a thin cock that just managed that.

Although the Dark Angel himself had started barebacking me two sessions previously, he apparently had insisted that all his guests had to wear condoms, which they did, and then just rolled them off and threw them on the floor when they were done. One smart aleck took it upon himself to ring out the count as each one hit the floor. I stopped listening to the count and gave up hope after the eighth one.

All the time the Dark Angel was standing nearby, watching me closely, and I fully understood this was some sort of testing of my surrender to him. So, I endured it and just let them manhandle and manipulate me like I was a rag doll, a docile rag doll with a well-fucked hole.

The apparent height of the evening for these dudes was when one produced the latest toy he had found. It looked like just a few interlaced small plastic tubes with a long plastic strip to me. But then, as a burly guy got behind me on the bed and got me in a full Nelson while my legs were cuffed up and out wide to the metal crooks, I realized it wasn't just a simple little collection of plastic tubes. At the base was a ring, similar in size—and function, I was soon to find out—to the base of the penis plug I had been forced to wear. He took my penis in his hand and pushed the head through the ring until it fit tightly at the rim of the head. There was an attachment in this that came over the glans and pushed down into the now-enlarged piss slit. I could see that this had an electrode on it, and for the first time, I began to squirm and raise objections—all of which the men in attendance thoroughly enjoyed.

There was another, bigger ring at the other end of the plastic line attached to this devise, and now the dude who had the biggest and thickest cock of all of the Dark Angel's guests and who hadn't fucked me up to this point brought his cock close to mine and pushed his cock through the ring. There now was little give, about nine inches, perhaps, in the line attaching his cock to mine.

I soon learned what this toy would do, as with the guy behind me still holding my arms and torso captive and all of the other guests huddled around and licking their chops, my assaulter rolled on a condom and then fed that big cock into me and began to stroke me. When his cock bottomed out in my asshole, the line pulled tight and set off the electrode in my piss slit, so that with each deep ramming, a small electric shock buzzed through my penis.

Not only was the hulking biker big and thick, but he also was an endurance fucker, and I had almost passed out from the rhythmic electrical shocking before he had shot his load inside me.

When they at last had done with me and tromped out of the bedroom in search of more beer, I sprawled totally exhausted and spread-eagled on the bed. I was shivering and trembling and probably would have been sobbing if I had had the energy to do so.

But the Dark Angel was still there. He jerked me off the bed and dragged me to the bathroom and told me to have another good piss. After I was done, he pulled me back into the bedroom and slung me down on the bed. He came down on the bed himself and replaced the penis plug. Then he pulled me to the floor and hog-tie cuffed me again and dragged me back to the cage through a pile of used condoms.

When the Dark Angel returned to the bedroom hours later, after his last guest had departed, there was no energy left in me at all—indeed, I had been just a quaking blob huddled in a wire cage for some time.

He let me out of the cage and removed all of the cuffs and the penis plug from me and let me use the bathroom again, and then, when I returned, he hooked my legs back up to the apparatus and fucked me to his release. All the time he was humming.

He turned tender then, my having, I would guess, passed his domination test. We showered together, me being so weak that he had to hold me up and run the washcloth over me. And then he took me to the other bedroom, one not littered with the evidence of my ravishment, and took me into his bed, hugging me tight to him and quickly going to sleep.

I, however, didn't sleep for hours, regardless of how exhausted I was. For the longest time, I huddled there with a phrase going over and over in my mind, a phrase that I couldn't even begin to understand: When he calls, I will come. It's what I want.

My Dark Angel snuggled up behind me, holding me in a vice grip with one sinewy arm around my chest, I caught a flash of light off of steel in morning light streaming through the curtainless windows. My cock cupped in his other hand, cold steel at my piss slit, invading, filling. Fully possessed. Moaning.

Career Guidance

"What is this shit?" Bernie Wasserman grabbed up tabloids in both fists and threw them across his desk at his client, who sat slouched and defiant in a club chair on the other side of the big mahogany desk.

"Those stories are exaggerated. I didn't know she was a man."

"Good god, Danny," Wasserman continued to bluster. "You are playing parts of a sixteen-year-old still. Caught being fucked by a transvestite in the back of your Hummer. What were you thinking? And a Hummer, god almighty. Who told you you could buy a Hummer? Your fans think you're riding bicycles. I didn't sign off on any of those bills."

"I'm almost nineteen," Danny blustered defiantly. "I don't have to tell you about every job I go out on anymore—or everything I buy with my own money."

"You sure as hell do have to tell me about every job you do, Danny Delmonte," Wasserman yelled. "I've got your contract. I get a piece of any paycheck you get. I've represented you since you were ten. I own your ass."

"That's it, isn't it?" Danny shot back. "This is all because I moved out when I was eighteen. You'd convinced my folks to let me live with you, and you were just licking your lips, playing it safe and waiting to fuck me when I turned eighteen—and I moved out instead."

"No, Danny," Wasserman said in a carefully controlled tone after taking a minute to pull himself together. "This is about your life. I've been lenient with you—and you've lived high on the hog. You've been spending it as fast as you make it. You've got maybe two more good years in your category and then it's iffy if you can transition to anything from the child roles. Very few are able to. And whoring around and getting high and making a fool of yourself in public isn't going to get you there. You need to come back under control. You need to move back in with me."

"No. You just want to get me in bed," Danny spat back. "And I'm going to beat that drug rap. The lawyer you got for me says it's a slam dunk."

"And what are you going to say about being caught in the backseat of a vehicle with a male prostitute in a car you weren't supposed to be driving as a condition of your release on the drug charges? Tell me about that. Tell me how happy the Children's Express Theater is going to be with this now if you sign this contract." Wasserman was waving a thick sheaf of paper that constituted a contract for three high school musicals.

"Fuck that. Fuck you. Fuck it all," Danny muttered as he sank down into his chair.

"This is your future," Wasserman said, his voice ominous and full of venom. "This is the only contract we have on the table. You already were aging out of these roles and now you've really fucked yourself with this stuff you are feeding to the tabloids. You are out of control. Do I tear up this contract and show you the door, or do we start this conversation all over again with you saying 'yes, sir' to me?"

Silence for a long minute with Danny looking at the floor. But his eyes came up fast enough at the sound of the tearing paper. Wasserman had torn apart one of the tabloid newspapers, though, instead of the contract.

"That got your attention, didn't it?"

Danny mumbled something into his chest.

"What? I didn't hear you."

"Yes." Just getting that word out seemed to be torture for Danny.

"Yes, what?"

Another moment of silence and then a muttered "Yes, sir."

"Stand up."

Danny looked up, he eyes showing confusion.

"I said stand up. And strip."

"What?" Now Danny was shocked.

"You said you were off the drugs. I don't know if I believe you."

"I never was on drugs—well not that kind," Danny said, his voice still showing his shock. And maybe a bit of fear now too.

"If not, then I won't find any marks on your body, will I?" Wasserman declared. "I can maybe clear this up—but only this last time—if you haven't fucked up your life more than just what's in these tabloids. If you're shooting up, you won't pass the studio tests and it doesn't matter if you sign these contracts or not. If not—and if I'm convinced you're not shooting up—I can get a doctor to say you were on prescription medicine because you were overworked and headed for a breakdown and that this is what has caused your behavior—but that you are back on the road to full recovery now. That always goes down OK in this town for at least the first time. So, if you want this contract, strip now and I'll check you out."

Danny looked all of the vulnerable sixteen-year-old role that he played so well as he meekly stripped down and stood there, naked, shivering slightly. He was a beautifully well-formed man—but still boyish looking, still about to pass as a teenager.

Wasserman sat behind his desk and looked Danny up and down as Danny's head hung in embarrassment and his hands crossed over his privates.

Wasserman opened a drawer in his desk and took out a couple of items and then, on his way around the desk, he dragged over a Chippendale straight-back dining room chair and plopped it down between where Danny was standing and trembling a bit, as if it was cold in Wasserman's office—which it wasn't—and his desk.

"Here. Sit," Wasserman commanded.

Danny looked up in confusion and just stood there.

"I said sit. And what do you say?"

Danny mumbled something, and Wasserman pushed the young actor down on his bare butt on the chair cushion. "What? I didn't hear you."

"Yes, yes, sir," Danny muttered. There were tears in his eyes now.

"This is all for your own good, Danny. You've gotten very cocky and beyond yourself. And you've lost control and you are this close to losing everything. And not just for you but for me too. I have given representation and career guidance priority to you for nearly ten years now. You need to learn control and discipline. You're fucking this up for both of us."

While he was saying this, Wasserman placed a wooden box and a couple of other items on a small cigarette table between the club chair and where he'd plopped the straight chair down.

To Danny's consternation and confusion, he was then strapping Danny's ankles to the front legs of the straight chair and pushing Danny forward, pulled his arms behind his back and tied his wrists together.

"What the . . . ?"

"Just shut up, Danny. You've been building up to this. It's time you understood who's the boss around here."

"God, Bernie, what . . . ?" The exclamation was set off because Wasserman was stripping off his own clothes now.

And then Wasserman, naked, was pushing himself in under Danny's buttocks and thighs and onto the seat of the straight chair. Danny was blustering and objecting in words that no child star even should know how to pronounce and then whimpering and pleading as Wasserman got his body below Danny's and Danny was lapped.

After he had lapped Danny and his engorging cock was running up the small of Danny's back, Wasserman reached over to the adjacent table and retrieved a condom packet, which he tore open, and a tube of lubricant. He rolled the condom on his cock and he began to diddle lube into Danny's asshole with one hand palmed under the young actor's butt and, after lubing up his own crowned cock, slicking up Danny's cock as well.

Danny was moaning and pleading and cussing up a storm. "I told you that you just wanted to fuck me," he muttered indignantly.

"Yes I've always wanted to fuck you, Danny. But I didn't. I was thinking of your career, though, and restrained myself. That's something you haven't done. That's something that you are going to have to learn if you are going to stay in this business. This is about so much more than wanting to fuck you."

"God, Bernie. You're driving me crazy." Bernie had lubed fingers up the young man's ass, loosening him up.

"Your tranny do this for you in the back of the Hummer, smart ass?" Wasserman asked darkly. "You're as loose as a two-dollar whore. How many other cocks have you had up there? Ones I didn't know about. Ones before me. Oh, yes I waited. But who didn't wait? Tell me, Danny?"

"Oh, God, Bernie, no. No, not many. None before I left your house. Oh, don't do this, Bernie. I'll behave."

"Who's the boss, Danny?" Bernie said.

"You are; you are the boss, Bernie . . . just don't . . ."

Bernie was lifting Danny's buttocks and hovering him over his erect phallus, the bulb of which was touching the rim of Danny's hole. Danny was panting and whimpering. "Who's your daddy, Danny?"

"What?"

"Who's your daddy, I said."

"You. You. You, sir."

"No 'sir' now, Danny. Say it. Call me Daddy."

"Daddy. Daddy. Oh, no . . . oh my god, noooooo."

Wasserman was pulling the younger man down onto his cock, slowly bringing him down, as Danny groaned and moaned and writhed within the close embrace Wasserman had him in. At length, he was bottomed—fully skewered—and defeated. He just sat there in Wasserman's lap, fully impaled, moaning softly, tears streaming down his cheeks, collapsed.

But he had taken all of Wasserman with a minimum of effort. Danny wasn't anything close to a virgin—and this ticked Wasserman off. He had wanted to be the first and had waited and schemed for it for years.

"Who was the first, Danny? Who? Tell me."

Danny was moaning but Wasserman lifted the young actor's buttocks half way off his cock and slammed him back down, and Danny yelped and struggled out an answer. "Sid, Sid Soltan."

"Soltan? The director of your last movie. When? When, Danny? And where?"

"My eighteenth birthday. In his studio trailer. He said he'd replace me in the movie if I didn't let him fuck me."

Now Wasserman was upset—really upset. "Why that old fart," he thought. "All of my plans and he sweeps in with a trump card."

Wasserman sat up very straight in the chair, forcing Danny to arch back into his chest and Wasserman's cock to be driven deeper into him. Danny groaned. "It's all for our own good," Wasserman was growling in Danny's ear. "You were running away. Weren't paying attention. Completely out of control. You need discipline. You need control. You need to be dominated. Is that right, Danny?"

Danny was sobbing quietly.

"I said, is that right, Danny? Aren't I right?"

"Yes . . . yes, Daddy," Danny murmured through his tears.

"You've been ass fucked before lots of times," Wasserman said, "enough to make the papers. There has to be something else, something more, to impress on you who is the boss here, who dominates."

"Please . . . please, Daddy," Danny muttered.

Then his eyes got really big and his body tensed and went rigid as he watched Wasserman open the wooden box on the table to reveal a series of size-graduated silver medical instruments—wands with slight bulbing at the tips—long, thin phalluses—arranged neatly in indentations in a blue-velvet foundation.

"What? What?" Danny's voice was filled with question and fear.

"The instruments of discipline . . . of ultimate domination, Danny," Wasserman said in a low, hoarse voice. "I want you to understand. I don't want to ever have to do this again—not as long as you have a career. Consider this career guidance. The best lesson you will ever learn from me; your salvation in being able to prolong your career. Your utter understanding of who is in charge here."

"No, please . . . don't, Daddy. I'll be good. I'll . . . Oh, nooooo."

"Hold still. Hold perfectly still. But not rigid. It will be much easier if you are relaxed. But very still. Very, very still."

Danny was whimpering again and Wasserman couldn't feel him breathing he was holding so still. Wasserman had taken one of the smaller wands out of the box and was holding it in front of Danny's terrified eyes.

"Breathe," Wasserman commanded. "Don't hold your breath. You won't be able to hold it as long as we'll be working here. We will be at this for a while."

"Noooooo," Danny whimpered.

When Wasserman had come under Danny, he had lifted the young man's arms over his head, so that Danny was stretched out against Wasserman's chest, his tied wrists at the back of Wasserman's neck. With his ankles shackled to the chair legs and his ass fully impaled on Wasserman's cock, Danny was sitting close in Wasserman's lap with little or no room to wiggle.

"Oh, nooooo, pleeaasee," he cried out as Wasserman ran the tip of the wand around Danny's nipples and then down the young man's belly, toward his crotch, as he cupped Danny's cock in the other hand, holding it at an angle jutting up from Danny's belly.

Danny began to pant and moan and sob for mercy as soon as Wasserman maneuvered the tip of the wand to Danny's piss slit and began to carefully insert it, sounding the young man's urethra in possibly the most intimate and dominating sex act one man can perform on another.

His cock deeply impaling Danny's ass, Wasserman was, in effect, fucking Danny's piss slit as well—or at least he was fully doing this when, after running the wand into the urethra channel nearly three inches, he began to slowly push it in and out.

Danny was moaning for real now, and gurgling sounds were coming up from deep inside him and he was holding very still but trembling and gasping and noisily taking in huge breaths of air.

"Who's the boss, Danny?" Wasserman asked in a low tone.

"You. You are, Daddy," Danny answered in a gaspy voice.

43

"And when I say you are to do something, what will you do?"

"Oh, god, oh god. Please stop. I think I'm going to come."

"No, no, you're not going to come, Danny. Daddy will tell you when you can come."

Wasserman slowly extracted the wand and laid it back in the case and picked another one of a larger size, and, ignoring Danny's pleas, began fucking the young man's piss slit with it in the same manner as he had done with the thinner wand.

"What will you do if I tell you to do it, Danny?"

"I'll . . . I'll . . . do it . . . Daddy. Ohhhhhhhh."

Wasserman brought his free hand up and cupped Danny's chin, arching the young man's head back into the hollow of his neck. He reached up with his thumb and pushed it between Danny's lips. "Suck this," he commanded. And Danny pulled the thumb into his mouth and gave it suck.

"This is it. This is how much I dominate you, Danny. Fucking you in all three orifices. No one owns you like I do, do they?"

"No . . . no, Daddy," Danny murmured in a thumb-strangled voice.

"And you will come home with me now—after we have signed these contracts—and I will fuck you whenever I want. And only me. And you will act the perfectly behaved, chaste child actor to the world. Right?"

"Yes . . . yes, Daddy . . . Oh. Ohhhh. I can't hold on any longer. I have to . . . come."

"Yes, you may come now, Danny," Wasserman said. And as he pulled the wand out of Danny's piss slit, the young man's cock burbled up in white fluid and he came in four jerks.

Danny was panting hard and Wasserman felt him relaxing and collapsing on his body.

Wasserman reached over and exchanged the wand for a larger-sized one.

Danny cried out in fear and frustration, knowing now that the ordeal was not over, but he was reduced to soft whimpering and shallow pants as Wasserman moved through two more sizes of wands and a second coming by Danny and until he felt there was no resistance in Danny at all anymore.

"I think we've made our point now," Wasserman said at length.

"Yes, Daddy," Danny murmured.

Wasserman laid the wands back on the table next to the chair. Then he took Danny's waist in his hands and lifted his torso up once, twice, three times, slamming the young man's torso down hard on his cock each time, with Danny giving a little cry of pain-mixed ecstasy with each deep thrust.

"OK, I'm going to unbind you now and I want you to reverse on my cock and face me and I want you to fuck yourself on my cock. Of your free will. You do that and we'll sign those contracts and get on with our life—together. If not, your career is over. Do you understand?"

"Yes, Daddy," Danny whispered in a voice of resignation.

And then, after he was unbound and turned himself in Wasserman's lap, Danny proved what a good actor he was by fucking himself to Wasserman's ejaculation—and giving an Academy Award performance on selling that he couldn't get enough of his master's cocking.

Searching for It

"Yo, there, buddy. Lookin' for somethin'? Cause I got somethin' for you."

Corbin took a good look at the burly man who had materialized from behind a stack of metal barrels beyond where the light over the alley door into the Christopher Street bar reached. He took a good look, reaching a quick decision because of the overly friendly way the man was extending a hand toward him.

"Ummm, no, I don't think—"

"I could show you a real good time. A tasty little trick like you."

"Sorry, just made a wrong turn back there," Corbin mumbled and backed out of the alley and into the street-lit gay bar district just up from the Manhattan docks.

He stumbled up the street, toward the upper end of the strip. That was where it was. Back there in the alley. He was sure of it. But it was a bad idea to come down here again. What did he think he'd find? And what did he think he wanted to get out of it if he did find it.

"Got a light?" The man was older, maybe in his forties. He'd been quite a looker in his day. Still not too bad. But there was no way he was right. He was built well enough, but not built like Corbin was looking for. Corbin didn't even have to think about seeing it. He was OK . . . and on a normal trip down here . . . maybe before what had happened, what Corbin was now

47

obsessed with finding . . . it would be just fine. But this wasn't what Corbin had come down to Christopher Street to find.

"Aw, come on. I can pay well for the right service. Up front. And I've got a room. It's a nice room. Clean and just here. Just over there across the street." He gestured toward the Christopher Hotel. Corbin knew it well. He knew it had recently been refurbished and the rooms indeed were clean and better than most here on the strip—certainly better than one of the back rooms in most of the bars here. And better even than the one he'd been in three nights ago.

"I was just ready to leave . . . to go on home," Corbin answered. But that wasn't true. He hadn't checked out more than three bars yet and he had been determined to walk the whole strip tonight until he'd found what he was after. He'd steeled himself for this for two day. Had wanted it again for two days. Had thought about little more than having it again, even though it made him shudder to even think about it.

The man came up close and put an arm around Corbin's waist, loosely though, as if not wanting to push him . . . too much . . . but not wanting him to bolt away either.

"Come on, sweetheart," the man whispered in Corbin's ear. "Good money and I give a good ride."

He smelled clean and the musky scent of his cologne was intoxicating. He felt firm. Trim and well dressed. He probably did have a fat wallet.

"I was going to go home. I just wanted to look in at a couple of more bars and then call it a night." It was true that he was going to check some more of the bars—at least that was what he'd planned to do before the encounter in the alley. That had unnerved him a bit. Too much like the other night, but not the right one. Not the right one at all.

"I can ride all night, and good money each time," the man murmured. "You're sweet. The best I've seen down here all night. You want to go into bars, I'll take you into bars. Give you whatever you want to drink. Here's Joey's right here. Come on in and let me buy you a drink."

It had been Joey's Corbin had been in three nights previously, and he indeed had planned to go in there to check. He had had high hopes that that was where he'd find what he was looking for. He'd come all this way down here—ignored what he should do. Go to the police is what he should do. But he'd built up courage to come down here. It would be a pity to cut and run now.

"Well, maybe just one drink. Here in Joey's."

When they entered the bar, Corbin's eyes scanned the room. Not many in here tonight. Very few of the build he thought was right. Several turned their faces toward him and smiled as he came through the door with his smooth-talking, well-dressed forties guy. The men always smiled for Corbin, and most showed interest. The forties guy put a hand on the small of Corbin's back and guided him toward the bar, his eyes also sweeping the room, challenging, claiming territorial rights.

Corbin continued to look, but what he wanted to see was the right-hand wrist of any guy who was anywhere close to the right build. He wasn't seeing what he was looking for.

Later, Corbin was thinking that the refurbishment of the Christopher Hotel hadn't really changed a couple of things that probably should have topped the list in getting fixed. The bedsprings still made that tinny, irritating grating sound and the headboard still thumped against the wall.

The forties guy had been right. He sure could ride. And he could get back in the saddle fast. Corbin lay on his stomach, naked, on the white chenille-covered bed, his hips raised to give the forties guy, knees clutching Corbin's thighs and fists pressing in the hollows below Corbin's shoulder blades, a good angle to bottom out as he seemed to want to do as he rode Corbin's ass.

The guy was good and the cock was thick and long enough, and Corbin didn't have any trouble giving him the gasps and groans and the usual "Yes, fuck me just like that" and "Give it to me good, Daddy," phrases that were expected of him, as he bunched up folds of the coverlet in his fists and thought about what he'd hoped to find down on Christopher Street tonight. And it wasn't this. But this was safe . . . a lot safer than the other. And maybe he could build up the courage to give it another try in the next couple of days.

* * * *

49

Ethan had never been in New York before, and the buildings soaring overhead, picked out majestically in the gathering twilight, exhilarated him. In fact, having grown up in Vancouver, British Colombia, he had never been on this side of the continent before, having signed on as crew for Ted Gleason's yacht and pretty much just sailed between Gleason's interests in the United States, most of them in Boston, and his preferred home in Bermuda.

What Ethan did know as he was tying off the bow of the yacht to the pier in the shadow of Manhattan skyscrapers is that he wanted to get laid—and bad. When he'd signed on with the *Seaskipper* crew, it was Liam, one of his fuck buddies from the fishing fleet in Vancouver, who had gotten him this cushy job on the yacht. He had enticed Ethan to follow him and he'd been taking care of Ethan's needs. And he'd done a great job of it—so good that Ted Gleason wanted Liam to take care of his needs too, and now Liam was laid up on land in Bermuda as manager of Gleason's estate.

Ethan had been four days on the *Seaskipper* without getting any. Liam had told him, with a wink, though, that he'd helped take the yacht to New York before, and that all Ethan needed to do was walk up a street called Christopher Street from where the yacht would tie up and he'd get all of the taking care of he needed. Ethan sure hoped so.

He didn't know what guys wore for cruising in New York—or how they signaled their need. But another guy on the crew had warned him that he'd probably not want to wear his working duds—baggy white cargo shorts, hanging low at the waist; a white cut-off T-shirt, showing his hard-muscled midriff; white deck shoes; and gold stud earrings—around this area of the city if he didn't want to get hit on. And so that's exactly what he wore. He just tied off his auburn hair in a ponytail and didn't bother to shave his four-day-old beard—mostly because it made him look older than his nineteen years, and he didn't want guys passing him by thinking he was too young—and started walking up Christopher Street from the docks as soon as he saw where it opened up from the water.

He had been warned correctly. He basked in the cat whistles he heard as he sauntered up the street. A group of three black guys waved at him from across the street and started to cross. Ethan had no experience with black guys—and he didn't like the idea of there being three of them—so he waved and shrugged as if he was meeting someone, and then turned and entered the closest bar door to him. A flashing neon sign over the door told him it was Joey's Bar. The black silhouette of a well-built guy was slouching against the "J" of the bar name with his back, so Ethan figured he'd guessed right on what sort of bar this was. As soon as he entered, he knew he was right.

The light was dim, the music was loud, and there was smoke reflecting in the roving multicolored beams of light revolving around the room, which gave the initial impression that the bar was crowded. But when Ethan's eyes adjusted to the dark, he could see that that wasn't so. Still, most of the attention of the men in the room—of those who weren't already far into making moves on each other—became focused on him.

The three black guys entered the bar and Ethan moved defensively away from the bar and farther into the area with tables as the three bellied up to the bar and, after voicing their drink orders to a bartender, turned toward the room. All three of them were staring at Ethan and smiling. Ethan moved back farther into the table area, until a hand reached out, gripped his wrist, and pulled him into enfolding arms.

"Hello there, sailor," a deep, gruff voice rumbled from the dimness. Ethan found himself drawn into the lap of a bulky, big-boned, heavily muscled bruiser of a man in jeans and a black muscle T-shirt. The man's strong arms encircled him and held him close. Even before more could be said, Ethan could feel the hardness of the man's staff rising at the cleft of his buttocks. The cargo shorts were light-weight material. Part of his Bermuda duds. A large, strong, calloused palm was pressing on Ethan's belly, holding him firmly in place. "Playing sailor today, are we?"

"I *am* a sailor," Ethan muttered defensively, gasping from the suddenness of being imprisoned. He turned his face toward that of the other man, seeing him more clearly with each passing second as his eyes adjusted to the light. The man was ugly as sin. His features were severe, bordering on gross. He was bald but he had dark, bushy eyebrows that made it look like he was permanently glowering. There was a wild look about the dark eyes,

51

his nose had been broken and badly reset, and there was a scar that sliced down from the corner of an eye and across both of his thin lips. His chin jutted. But while he was ugly and thuggish, he had the air of power and "able to have what he wanted" about him.

"Oh, a real sailor, then. Not Navy?"

"No. I work a private yacht," Ethan answered through heavy breathing.

"Too bad. Navy guys fuck well; usually have well-used holes."

Ethan squirmed to get up, but the man held him fast.

"Calm down," the man muttered. "You came in for this, didn't you? Or did you come in with those guys at the bar staring you down?"

"No, I didn't come in with them."

"And don't want to be with them, I guess."

Ethan didn't answer. But his trembling probably answered for him.

"You'd rather be with me, wouldn't you? Black guys are known for big dicks, but I bet mine will do you just as well."

Ethan didn't answer that either. He had been squirming, but he could feel that that was only arousing the man—and he knew he couldn't break the guy's grip anyway—so he settled down.

"Yes, good. Just quiet down. You a working piece?"

"Excuse me?"

"Did you come in here to pick up a john? You fuck for pay?"

"No," Ethan made his answer sound wounded without the least bit of acting.

"But you did come in here to get fucked, didn't you? Comin' in a bar like this, dressed like that. You came in to get laid. Feel that? Like that?" He was moving Ethan's butt around in his lap, letting him get the feel of the hardening cock. A hand had gone up under the hem of Ethan's cut-off T-shirt too and had found a nipple. His face was close in to Ethan's ear and he was licking the side of Ethan's neck under his ear lobe. All Ethan could think of was that he didn't think he could kiss the guy on the mouth. No, that wasn't all. He also was very much aware of the strength of the hardening cock he was sitting on. Ethan wasn't a large man—it seemed to him he was only half the size and weight of the big bruiser. He could barely touch the floor with the balls of his feet. But when he did so and tried to rise a bit out of the bruiser's lap, he was pulled back down, hard on the hardness of the man's tool.

Ethan moaned, which the man chose to take as a vote of appreciation for the feel of his cock.

"You want me to fuck you or do you want me to walk you over to those three black dudes at the bar? They look like they want to give you what you came in for too, but times three. Bet they could try to double you."

Ethan looked at the bar. The black guys were still watching him—closely. They weren't making any moves of approaching the table, however, even though there were three of them. This only added to Ethan's feeling of being overpowered by this man. Three well-built guys and they were just hovering there, watching.

"I . . . I don't . . . know. Here?!" he burst forth with, as he felt the man working on the knotting of his belt.

"Maybe here, yes. Maybe no. But you're going to sit on my cock and ride it like a good little boy, ain't you?" His hand moved to grab and squeeze Ethan's cock through the material of the cargo pants. "Or do you want me to give you to those black dudes?"

"No . . . I mean yes."

"Yes, what?"

"I want you to fuck me."

"You want to ride Daddy's cock?"

"Uh . . . yes." Ethan's eyes were on the black guys at the bar. They still were watching. He was panting shallowly now. The man was stroking his cock through the material of the shorts—and the man's cock was rhythmically pushing between his butt cheeks.

"Yes, what? Say it."

"I want to ride your cock, Daddy."

"Good. See what's on the table top right here?"

Ethan looked down at the surface of the table. There was a sheaf of condom packets beside a half-full beer mug.

"Oh. Please."

"I want you to open one of those rubbers and put it in my hand."

With trembling fingers, Ethan picked up the sheaf and pulled one packet away. He was shaking so badly that even with two hands it was hard for him to slit open the packet.

The man laughed and brushed the packet out of Ethan's hands. "Just testing you. Seeing how much you wanted it. But we'll play a bit."

The hand that had brushed the packet away was on Ethan's bare knee and began working its way up Ethan's thigh, up under the wide leg opening of the baggy cargo pants. Ethan could feel the metal of a ring on the man's finger—and he felt something else there, but couldn't quite figure out what it was. The hand was going under the hem of the pouch of the jock strap he was wearing when the man turned Ethan's face to his with his other hand and pushed a thick tongue between Ethan's lips. Ethan gasped and almost choked, but the man maintained his possession, his control of Ethan's mouth.

The other hand had reached Ethan's cock, flesh on flesh, and it was slowly stroking him hard. Ethan involuntarily was moving his hips, pressing and then releasing on the man's covered cock. He suddenly wanted the cock inside him. This is what he'd come for. It didn't matter that the man was ugly, Ethan could tell that he had a monster cock and could do him well.

Ethan's mouth was freed and he gasped at the arousing sensations he was being given below the waist.

"What'yer three lookin' at," the man's voice bellowed out. "This one's taken. Go find your own pigeon."

Ethan turned his face to the bar. The three black guys looked angry. But they also looked defeated. Two of them downed their drinks and then joined the other one who was already half way to the door.

"Please," Ethan murmured.

"Please what?"

"Please. Fuck me"

The man laughed a low, husky laugh. "Here and now?"

"If you want. But soon. Please."

"So, you want me to make you come?"

"Yes. Yes!"

The man laughed again. Then he retook possession of Ethan's mouth with his. The man's mouth tasted like stale tobacco and booze, but Ethan didn't care anymore. He'd come here to get a good fuck, and this man would give him that. A back room? a fleabag hotel room? right here? It didn't matter. Not as long as he could cock as well as he could make Ethan want it.

But then Ethan was shuddering and trying to pull away to gasp and object and ask what the hell was going on. The strange feeling of the hand coming up his leg. It must have been the underside of the ring on the guys finger. A metal bead. A big one. Being pressed in his piss slit.

The man held him fast in a strong hold, with one arm encasing his torso, a thumb and finger pinching Ethan's nipple. Ethan's mouth fully possessed. A hard cock between his butt cheeks, pressing at his hole even between the layers of intervening material. And the big bead on the underside of a ring pressing into his piss slit. Releasing and pressing. Releasing and pushing in. Rhythmically fucking his piss slit.

Ethan came in a pent-up spouting of cum and collapsed in the man's arms.

The man laughed another deep-chested, hoarse laugh and released his hold on Ethan so that the young sailor just sank into himself on the man's lap. The man reached over and tossed off his beer at one go, swept up the packets of condoms, and pushed Ethan off his lap. Ethan almost fell to the floor, but the man swung him around as he himself stood and dropped Ethan into the chair.

"Like piss slit fucking?" he leaned down and asked.

"It's . . . it's different," Ethan murmured.

"I asked if you liked it. There's more like that if you liked it. Did you like it?"

"Yes," Ethan answered truthfully, although he was a bit ashamed that he had liked it as much as he did.

The man took a couple of steps toward the bar exit.

"What? Are we . . . ?"

"Those guys are gone now. That's what you really wanted, isn't it? And you got to come. I got other things to do. Unless you want more of what you just got."

He laughed his way to the exit and was gone. Ethan just sat there, wilted. When he looked up, he saw that there were still guys interested in him. One, leaning at the bar and looking back at him, was a well-dressed, slim guy who was maybe in his forties. He'd obviously been a looker in his day, and he still looked like he was in good shape. He was dressed expensively. He lifted a glass and inclined his head like he was offering to buy a drink for Ethan.

They fucked in a back room of Joey's, with Ethan on the small of his back cross-wise on a massage table, and the forties guy holding his legs up and together with fists on his ankles while he pumped Ethan's hole vigorously with a fair-sized cock.

This was the fuck that Ethan had come for, but, even though this guy was handsome and had a good, strong stroke, the young sailor couldn't help but feel having been let down by the dangerous, ugly bruiser. And that fucking of his piss slit. He had never . . . ever . . . And the guy had teased him. Asked him if he liked it and maybe wanted more and when he said he did, just walked off.

* * * *

The forties man had released his legs and was pulling off his condom and releasing his seed on Ethan's stomach.

Ethan rolled to his right, ready to pull himself off the bed.

"Hey, wait. Where are you going? I told you $100 for two fucks. Roll onto your back. I'll be ready again in a few minutes."

* * * *

Ethan stumbled out of Joey's. He needed to piss, and he probably should have done it in the bar. But for some reason he just wanted to be gone. The forties guy was OK, but he wanted to exchange phone numbers and addresses and such, and Ethan wasn't into that. He still had the sour feeling in his stomach that the ugly guy had ruined his night. Ethan was $100 richer when that wasn't even required, but, despite what should have been two decent fucks, he felt unsatisfied. And it was all the big bruiser's fault.

He looked around to make sure those three black guys weren't still hanging around and then turned the corner and stood facing a wall beside a parked black van. He unzipped and pulled his dick out of the pouch of the jock strap and, leaning into the wall supported by the heel of the other hand of an outstretched arm, and pissed a strong-arced stream of piss against the cinder brick wall.

God, that felt good, he thought, as he shook the dick dry.

He didn't even have time to cry out as a hood was forced over his head and he was slung sideways through a van door and onto a carpeted floor. His wrists were being cuffed and his arms were being pulled over his head and attached to something. He heard the van door slide shut with a solid thump. The cargo shorts and then the jock strap were jerked down his legs, which were wishboned and raised, with strong fists grabbing his ankles.

He cried out inside the hood and arched his back, as a cock slid into Ethan's channel—with difficulty as it was thicker than the forties man's had been—but yieldingly as Ethan was lubed and opened up by the two recent fucks.

The man was breathing heavily and muttering something Ethan couldn't make out from inside his hood. Was he talking to someone. Were there others there? The three black guys?

But the cock was thick and long and was pumping him even better than the forties guy did. And longer. Almost interminably. Hands were moving up his torso, grabbing his pecs under the cut-off T, digging into his nipples, punishing him. Ethan cried out under the hood and his hips went into motion. This was a fuck! He was meeting the cock thrust for thrust, and he could feel the vehicle they were in rocking back and forth. The man's torso lowered to his. It was brushing up and down on Ethan's chest in rhythm with the thrusts of the man's cock.

Hairy. The chest was hairy. Chaffing Ethan's chest, but he didn't care. Bulging muscles. The man was strong. And vigorous. And long lasting. Or was it just the one. He would pull out and then thrust in again. Was that someone else taking over?

Ethan shot his load, and soon after, with a couple of jerks and a grunt and groan, the man's body tensed and he too came. Ethan felt no flow inside, so he must have been capped. It was almost a disappointment. Ethan wanted to feel the creaming of his insides. But maybe it was for the best. Maybe it meant Ethan wasn't in mortal danger. Or maybe the man was just protecting himself.

He was left there, where he lay, his wrists bound above his head, a hood covering his head, when he heard the van door slide open and then close, another door open and close, and then the van was on the move.

* * * *

Ethan decided they must be in a bathroom. His knees, painfully were on a hard, tiled floor. His belly was on the cold rim of a porcelain tub, and his arms were dangling in the tub, still bound at the wrists.

A man was hunched over him from behind and fucking him. It was a glorious fuck. If the floor and porcelain weren't so hard and cold, it would be an even better fuck. The hood was jerked off his head—and, sure enough, he was draped over the rim of a bathtub in a small and barely functional bathroom—and he gasped for air.

"Please," he pleaded when he could get his breath. "my knees. My belly. It's killing me. Please can we do this another way."

"But you want it, don't you?" The voice was muffled. Ethan managed to turn his head enough to get the impression, his eyes following the line of bulging muscles of an arm, of a massive, heavily muscled, and quite hairy—dark hair—chest. And a head covered by a hood. The man was tanned, but either white or Hispanic.

"Yes," he conceded. "I want it. But could we . . . ?"

The man laughed, that too muffled, but he pulled Ethan up and backed him the few feet it took to get to the opposite side of the room. He sat on the toilet and then brought Ethan down on his lap and onto his cock and resumed the stroking by lifting Ethan up and down on the cock. Ethan didn't fight it. He placed the balls of his now-naked feet on the tiled floor and helped with the rhythm of being raised and lowered on the cock.

His eyes free to see now, Ethan looked around. The bathroom was clean and neat—just small and old-looking. The man's thighs between his spread legs were tan and hairy. Black hair. The man had forced Ethan's arms up with Ethan's bound wrists locked behind the man's neck, which made Ethan arch his back, putting his torso in the form of a taut bow. When the man stopped raising Ethan up and down by his waist and felt that Ethan was willingly doing that himself by the leverage of the balls of his feet, the man's hands had gone to covering Ethan's pecs again and playing with his nipples. When he did that Ethan saw, for the first time, the tattoo on the man's wrist. He couldn't quite make out what it was, but he was working on it.

That was forced out of Ethan's mind, though, when the man raised his feet, massive, hairy-toed boats, to where his heels were on the rim of the tub across the room. This forced Ethan's shoulder blades back onto the bulging, hairy pecs of the man and lifted his feet off the floor. At this angle, the man's thrusts up into Ethan's channel, using the leverage of the man's heels on the tub rim, sent the cock ever deeper and Ethan was panting and groaning and moaning. And luxuriating in the exhausting fuck.

Ethan was totally exhausted after the fuck, but the man seemed as vigorous and hyper as ever. He stood up from the toilet and moved Ethan to where he was draped over his arms in front of him, Ethan laid across his arms, dangling like a rag doll, still panting softly from the total fuck, and looked up at the massive hairy chest and the bulging arm muscles. Ethan had never been taken by such a strong, beautifully built man as this before.

He was carefully carried into another room and laid on some sort of medical table. The man unbound his wrists but immediately bound them in cuffs on the edge of the padded table parallel to his shoulders. Ethan's feet were bound in stirrups that raised and spread them. His buttocks was raised by a wedge at the bottom end of the table.

Still wearing the hood and nothing else, the man then rolled a trolley up to below and somewhat beside the table. Ethan's eyes went from the massive tube of now-flaccid manhood dangling between the man's beefy thighs and to his right wrist, where Ethan could see the tattoo again, but still could not make out what it was. But his eyes also went back to the barrel chest, with the matting of black, curly hair, cascading down to his groin—and to the pronounced curves and bulges of all of the muscles and the armor-like plate of his six pack. Now that he could see the man's body completely, the line between the tan and that of the Speedo he must have been wearing when he was getting his tans revealed that he was a white man.

Ethan wished he could be free to let his hands roam on that body, to follow the tan line with his fingers, to taste that cock and watch it engorge, and to pull it inside him and ride it like a cowboy. And maybe after this . . .

But, what was that? What was the man doing? He had picked something up from the surface of the table he had rolled over. A long, thin, metal wand.

"Do you know what this is?" the voice, muffled by the hood, asked.

"No," Ethan murmured.

"It's called a wand. Do you know where it goes?"

"No."

"Think about that." The man had cupped Ethan's cock and raised it. The tip of the wand was lowered toward the tip of the cock. "Where could it go?"

"No. Noooo. Please no!" Ethan cried out.

"Ah, you've guessed it. Now you must hold very still. I tell you this for your own good."

"Noooo!"

The man slapped Ethan on the belly, and said in a more forceful voice. "I said you must hold still. You will thank me for warning you of that."

"Please don't," Ethan said with a whine. "Don't do this. Please. Why are you . . . ? Oh, shit. Nooo!"

He could feel the cold steel slowly enter his piss slit. Just a little way. Enough for him to realize that this was going to happen. He gasped and then whimpered, "Why?"

"I have enjoyed fucking you. I can tell you have enjoyed it too. We are going to be friends. Very intimate friends. And I am going to teach you control. Ultimate control. I liked the look of you from the very beginning. And dark hair. That five o'clock shadow. It completes the package. We'll have to keep that."

Ethan had been concentrating on trying to understand what the man was saying through the hood. If he hadn't been, he would have realized that the thin metal wand was nearly half buried inside him. He was trembling, but as warned, he was trying to remain as still as he could.

He gasped and moaned as the wand was slowly pulled out of his penis. He was going hard in spite of the horror of what was happening.

He looked down the line of his body and saw the man picking up a thicker wand. "Please . . . oh my god," he whimpered as the thicker rod entered his slit and slowly was pushed in.

"Just to this point and then just watch what happens," the man said. "You want it. You'll see."

Ethan looked down as the wand half buried in his raised penis. The man didn't have a hand on it, and yet it was moving. It was sinking into him. And he could feel it sinking in.

"See. Your cock wants it. It's taking it in on its own." Then the gasping and the sucking in of air as the wand was pulled out.

As the man was turned to the table, selecting a thicker wand, Ethan could see that the man was aroused by this. His cock, huge and curved up toward his belly, was hard again.

With the fourth wand buried three-quarters of the way inside Ethan's penis, the man pushed the stirrups Ethan's feet were tied to toward the base of the table so that his legs were bent. Ethan watched the man roll a condom on his cock. Then he placed his hands on Ethan's knees and moved in between Ethan's thighs and entered his channel with his cock.

Ethan sighed and moaned as the man slow-pumped him. The young sailor almost forgot that over four inches of a thick wand were buried in his penis. The man moved Ethan's knees back and forth with the rhythm of his stroking and Ethan became lost in the fuck. He was close to coming, when the man stopped and pulled his cock out. He stood there, holding Ethan's knees still, while Ethan's breathing slowly returned to normal and he lost the urge to ejaculate.

Then the man said, "Ultimate control," and Ethan watched in fear, renewed horror, and fascination as the man brought his cock head up to the exposed tip of the wand. He squeezed the head of his cock and the piss slit opened right up and then he swallowed two inches of the wand in the cock. One end of the wand was in Ethan's cock and the other end in the man's.

"The ultimate fuck," the man said. "You are mine now . . . unless . . ." One of his hands enveloped Ethan's balls and pulled and released them as more of his cock swallowed the end of the wand and the two cock heads came close together. The hand left Ethan's balls and moved down. Fingers entered Ethan's ass and worked their way in and out, stretching for the prostate.

Ethan arched his back and turned his head to the side and moaned deeply. The man started to move his penis, moving the metal wand back and forth in both Ethan's penis and his own, bringing the cock heads closer together.

"Oh shit yes. Oh fuck. Oh god, yes. Yesss," Ethan moaned.

"Do you want me to stop? To free you? To send you back to that yacht of yours?"

"Oh god no. Fuck me. Fuck me like this forever. Oh, shit . . . I'm going to come."

"Go ahead."

And Ethan did come, and so did the man, obviously having been able to hold himself for a mutual ejaculation, the cum of the two burbling out around the sides of the wand and lathering each other's cock bulbs.

The man leaned over Ethan and released his cuffed wrists. Ethan's hands immediately buried themselves in the silky chest hair of the man's pecs, hungrily seeking the man's taut nipples. The man pulled the hood off his head.

It was the bald-headed man who piss-slit fucked him with the bead of his ring in Joey's bar. It hit Ethan then that he should know this. The man had alluded to a different, more intense piss slit fuck than he'd given with the bead on the ring, and just now he'd revealed that he knew Ethan sailed on a yacht.

"Do you want to go home or do you want it again?"

Ethan didn't hesitate for a second. "Again. And again and again. Oh fuck yes!"

The man had begun to move his hips again, moving the wand connecting their penises back and forth inside them. "I'm ready if you are. But do you want to try a thicker wand?"

"Whatever you want," Ethan murmured between gasps and heavy pants, his hands greedily tugging at the man's nipples. "You are in control."

"Good answer. I knew you could accept that," the man said as he raised off of Ethan and moved his hand over to select a thicker wand.

Later, the man carried a totally spent Ethan down the hall and into a bedroom with four twin beds against the walls. A young blond man was on one of the beds. He was naked and his body was beautiful—slender but well-muscled. He had been reading a skin magazine, but he looked up, eyes flashing, as the man carried Ethan in.

"This here, the blondie, is Mark. Mark meet Ethan. He's going to be the dark headed one."

Without acknowledging Ethan, the blond turned his eyes on the man and raised up on his knees in a provocative pose. "You going to do me again now, Seth? Sound and fuck me again. I need you. I need you bad. I need the wand. The cock fuck. Please, are you—"

"Yes, Mark, I'm going to do you now." The man—who had now been named Seth—walked over and picked the blond up in his arms. "Bathroom's through there, and the kitchen is down the hall, darkie. Make yourself to home."

Ethan laid back on the bed he'd been placed on after picking up the magazine the blond guy had been reading. His eyes roamed the bodies and sexual positions of the guys on the glossy cover without seeing them as he heard the cries of passion from the blond in the room down the hall—wishing all of the time that it was him again. Not wondering where he was, how long this would last, or how he was going to get back to the yacht he should be sailing on to Bermuda in a couple of days. Only thinking of that steel rod joining his cock to that of the big, ugly, magnificent bruiser Seth and living vicariously what the mouthy blond in the other room was screaming was happening to him.

* * * *

When Corbin came out of the back room at Joey's after being fucked by the handsome forties guy with the open wallet, he

63

realized that this was the bar he'd been looking for. He had been three sheets to the wind when he'd left the bar that night and had been pulled into the alley and into that van and fucked like he'd never been fucked before in his life.

He'd never even heard about sounding before. After the hooded guy had done him and then sounded him and then pushed him out of the van and driven off, Corbin had gone home and researched it. It had taken him quite a bit of research to find that ultimate fuck—what the hooded man had called the "ultimate control"—but he'd found it eventually. The two-cocked sounding, with the dominant guy controlling the action of the mutual penis fuck. Nothing had been said about coming at the same time and slathering each other's dicks, but Corbin just couldn't get that out of his mind.

The man had been hooded. And so had Corbin been hooded. But Corbin's had come off during the fuck and he'd seen it—the tattoo on the guy's wrist. It was only after it was all over—the next day, in fact—that Corbin had realized that the tattoo depicted exactly what he now craved again. Two penises, their heads connected with a thick rod.

Corbin had to have it again. And again and again and again. He wouldn't recognize the guy by his face, but there couldn't be more than one tattoo like that on a man of magnificent, hairy build cruising the Christopher Street bars. It was just a matter of time and research.

Corbin bellied up to the bar and ordered a beer. Then he turned and surveyed the dimly lit room, with the colored beams of light roaming around. A yellow light highlighted the man at the table. It was only for an instant. But it was enough. He'd had his hand raised, and Corbin had seen the tattoo. Just in a flash, but enough.

They were at one of the tables. The big man had a younger, slender man, in his lap. A redhead, with freckles. But good looking and built nicely. The man was ugly as sin, but that didn't matter. That wasn't what Corbin wanted from the man. The redhead was being held tightly in the big man's lap and there was movement at their hips. The back of the redhead's head was pushed into the hollow of the big man's shoulder, black hair curling out of the neckline of the big man's T-shirt, and the younger man had the look of being in dreamland on his face. A pair of shorts and bikini briefs were laying at the feet of the redhead.

It was clear that the big man was lap fucking him. It was also clear to Corbin from memory, that, although the redhead's shirt was covering his lap, the position of one of the big bruiser's hands underneath the front of the shirt told Corbin that the bead on the underside of the man's ring was busy fucking the piss slit of the redhead's penis. And the redhead was loving it, without having any knowledge just how far that could be carried.

Corbin didn't want to watch this, but he didn't want to leave either. He'd wait until it was done and then he'd follow the big guy—at least get the license plate of his van. The redhead thought he was in heaven now, but if the big bruiser gave him the sounding treatment he'd be in higher glory yet. Corbin was already shaking in anticipation of getting it again.

But Corbin was not destined to be satisfied by the ultimate fuck again. Corbin was a blond. The big bruiser, Seth, already had a blond in his collection. Corbin was fine for a fuck and a sounding in the back of the van, but Corbin wasn't going to experience the ultimate—again and again—as he dreamed of.

Tonight, big Seth was shopping for a redhead for his collection.

Prepped and Sounded

Not for the first time I didn't like the gleam in Leon's eye or the lilt in his voice when he told me I had an assignment. He was much too pleased with himself when he handed me the envelope containing the address and the gate key. We'd been getting along better than usual lately—or had been up to the time he seemed to think that meant I was warming to him and he propositioned me again and I turned him down flat again. But if there was a little twist to this assignation, at least it would be short-lived. The address was right here in the city. The Gordan Institute up in the Hollywood Hills.

I knew this to be a tony private plastic surgery hospital for those who wanted to be recarved without losing sight of their swimming pools and movie star mansions. Not because I'd done anything like that myself, of course. I was still at my peak, thank you, very much, and wouldn't need any of that sort of help for a good ten years more. Depending, though, I guessed, on what I did between now and then to earn my pay—just how taxing earning that pay was. And when I did need plastic surgery, there was no way I was going to be able to afford the Gordan Institute, unless by then I'd acquired a sugardaddy who was will to pay through the nose to keep me young and supple looking.

I just hoped that Leon hadn't agreed to let me get sliced up.

"So, what costume?" I asked.

"Oh, just go as you are," Leon answered. And then he laughed. "Chances are you won't be wearing it long anyway."

I took the envelope from Leon's claws and gave him a wan "you don't intimidate me—much" smile and headed my Beamer convertible up slope. It was late afternoon on a Sunday and it was "another damn beautiful" day enhanced by the relative lack of bumper-to-bumper traffic.

I halfway knew where the Gordan Institute was, and I found it without too much trouble, hulking behind a high stuccoed privacy wall next door to what had once been Bela Lugosi's haunted manse. Leon had given me a plastic key card like they use for hotel room entry, and it opened up the iron gates at the institute a charm. No one was about as I drove in and parked next to a silver Mercedes convertible on an otherwise empty, bricked-over parking pad. By the time I got to the front entrance, hidden in the shadows behind a porte cochere, a covered entryway cars could pass under, no doubt designed for privacy in the arrival and departure of the well-heeled patients, the entry door was opening and I could see there was at least one other person than me here on a Sunday. The absence of other cars disturbed me a bit. This was a residential facility; was there some sort of law against rich people getting tummy tucks on weekends in May? I wondered.

"You were sent by the agency?" a well-modulated baritone voice asked from the depths beyond the opening door.

"Umm, yes. Alphonse?"

"Come in. Yes, yes, you'll do nicely."

I knew that. He didn't have to tell me that. They charged three thou an hour for my attentions. And for that I did quite a bit more than "nicely."

The door swung open, and I was facing "Alphonse." He wasn't really Alphonse. I knew that, and I'm sure he knew I knew that. His mug, no matter how many times it had been redone, was well known in town. He was Grant Gordan, the celebrated magic surgeon of beauty. This was his institute.

He was playing doctor. Starched, stark-white three-quarter-length doctor's smock over soft-cotton, institutional green scrubs that somehow still gave the impression they had been tailored and cost a bundle. Crinkling transparent plastic booties on what looked like gray bedroom slippers. He was tricked out to be playing the senior physician in a long-running television medical drama. Gray-haired, in his fifties, but handsome, and chiseled to an epitome of perfection that only a millionaire's billfold or an "in the business" discount could provide. A very nice bedside smile that, alone, would have cost me a fortune.

"Oh, excuse me," I stammered. "Did I get the day or time wrong? Have I interrupted a procedure?"

"No, no, of course not. You're right on time. No other procedures today. We're undergoing renovations this week, so no other procedures at all. No patients in residence."

"Oh, but—" I'd heard that "other" word twice. It didn't give me a warm fuzzy feeling.

"Oh, these. What I'm wearing. I was just trying on a new shipment of surgical wear. Dr. Gordan just had these sent in."

Hokay, I thought. It's your ten thou, "Alphonse," I thought. I had peeked at Leon's chart—as I always tried to do so I knew when I should be going off the clock. This guy had bought four hours and gotten a discount of two thousand for booking that block of time. This almost always meant at least a double, and not easy ones at that, but I was just as happy if they thought of that in advance and padded the time. Often trying to hammer a recharge and second fucking into an hour—or even two hours— became quite frustrating for the client and often played out in their attitude as something unpleasant.

"Follow me, please." And with that, "Alphonse" turned and walked briskly down a corridor leading off to the right of the plush reception room that, with its yawning stone fireplace, vaulted ceiling, and big expanse of glass overlooking a sea of green grass, majestic pines, and parts of the city looked more like the living room in a mountain lodge than a hospital waiting room.

I followed in the wake of the crinkling noise his surgical booties were making with the thought that, if I had known we were going to play doctor, I would have seen if Leon had a nurse's uniform in his wardrobe room.

I was ushered into a large, wood-paneled room with book-lined walls except for one well-lit panel that sported what I'm sure was meant to be an intimidating number of framed university diplomas, medical licenses, honorary plaques, and photos of

"Alphonse" shaking hands with various extremely well-preserved movie stars and industry titans of old—or at least of older than they had been made to appear.

The mahogany desk was massive, the throne behind it that "Alphonse" perched in momentarily was massive, and the sort of wheel chair contraption he waved my butt into was nothing short of strange. It was a comfortable chair and all that, but did he put his prospective clients into wheel chairs this early in the sales pitch? I didn't have time to let this thought percolate, however.

"I trust you've been told the scenario and the service."

"Ummm. No, actually," I said.

"Oh, well, then," Alphonse said. "I do have a contract, you know. And the money's been paid."

"Good, fine," I said. I couldn't think of anything else to say. I was busy racking Leon over in my brain. I knew there was a reason for that evil little smile. Holding the particulars back from me again. Such a poor loser.

By then, Alphonse had bounded back out of his—or, rather, Dr. Gordan's—throne and was moving around the room.

"Strip down, please. I want to see if my directions were followed."

I stood up from the wheel chair and started to take off my clothes, in the slow, provocative way I'd been taught to do, wondering all the time whether I was supposed to wear something I hadn't been told about. As I did so, Alphonse came around to the edge of the desk, facing me, and perched there, closely scrutinizing my every movement. I imaged that I was a client asking for a little more here and a little less there, and I wondered if he also was thinking about how I could be recarved to best advantage.

But his eyes were slitted, and he was humming softly to himself. From long experience, I recognized this as a sign of satisfaction with the goods.

"Ah, yes," he said when I was stripped down, giving out a sigh and letting his hand run across his crotch. "Nice body hair. And a natural blond, I see."

Well, no, but he didn't need to know all that was entailed in that. But I was pleased that even a master plastic surgeon could

70

be fooled by the job. It made me feel that the money I'd thrown at it was well worth the price.

"Sit, please."

I did so, and Alphonse was back on the move. He was behind me, and I heard the noise of something being dragged toward me. I looked around in time to see some sort of steel contraption on wheels, supporting a large cylinder rolling up to my chair. But that's all the time I had to see anything, as the doctor was right behind me then, throwing his arms around my chest, holding me down into the wheel chair with one arm and clamping a mask over my mouth and nose with the other. I struggled briefly, but not for long. The gas was fast and effective.

When I came to, I was strapped down on my back on a white-paper-covered vinyl operating table. My wrists were bound close behind my head, which pulled my arms up and close beside my head on either side. My ankles were bound too, but to flexible appendages that extended beyond the end of the table, which only reached to the small of my back. It was apparent that these appendages could be manipulated apart and up and even folded to bend my legs. It was obvious now why the wheel chair had been offered to me as a seat; it saved muscle power in getting my dead weight to the table.

I awoke to a whimper. It was mine.

"Ah, good, awake. Be aware that I contracted for the specific services I require. Including the control mechanisms."

I reminded myself once again to get Leon for this. Somehow, some way.

I focused on the voice. Alphonse—Grant Gordan—all smiles and standing over me with an aerosol can in one hand and in the other—a straight razor.

"Oh, God, no," I muttered. "Please—" That was Leon's game. Services that rarely were called for and that most would not agree to. I wondered whether I would have agreed to them myself. I think I'm known in the business as a big risk taker, but I didn't know if I would have agreed to this. And Leon didn't give me a chance not to.

"You must hold very still, or this will undoubtedly hurt you more than it does me," Gordan murmured. And then he smiled. I knew the look in those eyes. He was aroused.

71

He started squirting foam onto my torso and into my pits. It was cold, and I squirmed a bit. I said nothing; I was still assessing the situation and how and whether to get out of it. Just how crazy was he? Was this just the first stage of something? He lifted the razor and I stopped squirming. I wasn't that stupid.

He had music going on in the background. Just what I was used to hearing when I went into a dentist's office. And he was humming as he worked.

The razor moved from my right pit to my left pit. This was followed by Gordan's tongue, as he lapped up the residual lather there, which must have been something tasty other than soap, because he was having a good slurping time of it.

"You know," he said as he finished there and was carefully shaving around my nipples and along my hairline down to my navel, "For years I watched my patients being prepped by the nurses before surgery, and I never realized why I got a hard-on before surgery. For the longest time, I thought it was the surgery itself that was a turn on for me. And I was ever so grateful that I had gone into a profession that could give me so much pleasure in addition to paying me so well. But then I slowly caught on. I was aroused by the prep. The shaving and the cleaning off of the lather. Of course I found I liked other medical procedures too."

Prepped for what? I wondered. What other medical procedures? The man had said "services." What more than this was going to be required of me?

"I can show you a really good time without this, you know," I stuttered out. "I can give you a fuck like you've never had before." It was grabbing at straws. But I was worried about where this might lead. Whether he had even darker fetishes. I usually liked to be very sure of a client before I was tied up.

"Yes, yes, I'm sure—and perhaps you shall," Gordan said in a faraway voice, which told me that he was locked into his fetishes. "You know, though, that after I knew what it was that I wanted, I had a dilemma. I couldn't really take the risk of pursuing this on a real patient. Besides the fact that the operating room is full of people in this stage, there where phenomenal risks with the patient's lawyers. And few of my patients come in with a body as gorgeous as yours, which is doubly arousing to work with. So, you know—"

He had broken off because his mouth was full of foam and nipple now. He had shaved my chest, down to my navel and was cleaning up the lather with his tongue. He was really good at it, and I wondered how much practice he had had with this. How many before me? If other guys in my profession had gone missing, I think I would have known. The agency would have known. But, what if I were the first?

And what if it wasn't? What if this was Leon's ultimate revenge and he had taken such revenge on others who just weren't there one day?

I was so deep in worry and thought that I didn't know how long it had been since he'd stopped tonguing me down. When I looked around, I saw that he already had his scrubs off and was putting his white lab coat back on over his naked body. For his mid fifties, he really looked good. But, at the same time, too good. Plastic. I bet he'd had every inch of his body done and redone. And I wondered if they really could enhance a penis like that with plastic surgery. His body was hairless, so at least he carried this fetish of his through to himself.

He opened a condom package and crowned his pride and joy. Time for something I was more familiar with.

Gordan moved to below me, and I felt the lower appendages of the operating table, the arms to which my legs were strapped, being widened and bent so that I was in what I imaged to be the "birthing" position. Gordan was standing between my legs, and I saw the gleam of the metal aerosol can caught in the glare of the overhead operating lights.

Cold, wet. My pubes were being lathered up. And then my asshole too. I tensed up as I felt one of his fingers breaching my rim and pushing into at least the knuckle, taking lather with it. I did my best to relax as I looked down and saw the razor hovering over my pubes. I wasn't all that happy. I'd spent some time and money grooming and colorizing my pubes and it hadn't entailed being completely hairless down there.

I panted shallowly and tried to be professional and not whimper or beg as I felt the razor scraping across my groin. Gordan was fisting my cock with his other hand, holding it out of the way and stroking it up and down. I was involuntarily engorging. Which was fine. He'd paid for the service, and I would

73

give the service. If I was going to beef, it would be to whoever I could find in the agency above Leon. It would be no good to let Leon know I thought I had a beef about this assignment; he'd delight in listening to me whine. If I ever got home from this assignment, of course.

I watched Gordan's head come down to my groin and lick at the lather and then up the side of my cock, and he swallowed me and constricted his cheeks around my tool. I groaned and strung a series of appreciative-sounding yeses for him and started a shallow rhythm in my hips to let him know that his was a superior suck.

After a bit of this, he lifted off my cock but still held it in a fist as he lathered up my inner thighs and began to scrape and tongue again.

Then the razor wasn't scraping. The finger wasn't in my hole. I almost lifted up off the table as Gordan thrust his cock inside me, running thickly and deeply at the first thrust, his entry smoothened by the lather he'd shot up into me.

The shave was finished. He was fucking me in deep thrusts, fully aroused by his fetish, ready to finish off the surgical fantasy.

I knew this part. I cried out for him, telling him how good he was and how I wanted it never to stop, and Gordan rode with it. Thrusting and thrusting and thrusting. Making animal noises, while I moaned and groaned and told him he was killing me but not to stop.

He was as good with his cock as he had been with his razor. And I was enjoying this part—but doing all I could to make him enjoy it too. Enjoy it far more than the shaving part and certainly far more than any part he might be planning to proceed to after this. I wanted him to want me to be giving him the best of times and wanting me back some other time. Not carrying on with any possible terminal plans in this session.

With an exclamation, Gordan pulled out of me, jerked off the condom and shot up over my balls onto my now-smooth groin.

I sighed deeply and collapsed back onto the paper sheeting, only then realizing that I had arched my back to meet him thrust for thrust in his wild, exuberant fucking.

I did everything I could to act like what we had done was totally exhausting, if totally wonderful—for both of us—and that we had done what we were going to do. But then I looked up at the clock on the wall and realized that he had nearly two hours left on his contract. I groaned, and this time it didn't have anything to do with sex.

I refocused on Gordan. He was opening another condom packet. This time he rolled the condom onto my cock, which, conveniently, was standing at full attention and was hard as a rock. He let loose another cloud of lather on my capped tool.

Then, moving real well for his age, Gordan came up onto the operating table and knelt, straddling my hips, facing me. He held my cock rigid while he slowly encased my cock with his channel and began to slowly ride me. I gave him a good time and appropriate sounds of pleasure and, in the end, a good feel of the bulb of a condom billowing forth to capacity well up his canal.

I wondered if the clock had stopped. He still had more than an hour when we were done with that. He went back to the razor and the lather, and my legs and arms were completely denuded and exposed to the breezes.

We had come to what I thought of as the danger point, but this particular fetish of Gordan's turned out to have its limit. He left me alone then to recover—for both of us to recharge, I was to learn. I thought he'd release me then, having completed what he wanted to do early. But this wasn't the case. He was just moving on to another, far more intimate fetish.

I heard him coming down the hall, humming happily to himself. I also heard the wheels on some sort of cart. When he entered the room, I saw that he wearing a surgical coat but nothing else. He also was in half erection and was crowned with a condom, so I knew we were going to be having anal sex again. I had no idea what the cart was for. Laid out on top of the cart was a white towel and on top of this was a series of silver rods, of various sizes, laid out in graduated progression.

Soon thereafter—after he had put a ball gag in my mouth—I learned what the rods were for. By then I was trying, quite unsuccessfully, to writhe away from him and to tell him in no uncertain terms through the confinement of the ball gag that I wasn't in the least bit interested in doing this.

"Calm down and relax," he commanded as he took hold of my cock with one hand. He was holding one of the smaller silver rods in the other. "You'll want to be very still for this procedure, or you will damage yourself."

Damage myself? I wanted to scream. You're the one doing this.

"I specified the services when I contracted with your business," he went on to say. "They said there would be no problems. You won't be harmed if you hold very still. If you don't fight it, you'll enjoy it."

Fuck you, Leon, is what I was thinking.

I tried to relax as the tip of the silver wand was placed at the entrance of my piss slit, but I involuntarily tensed and raised my hips and held my breath as the rod slowly was twirled into my urethra channel. I groaned and started to pant as Gordan pulled it out an inch and then twirled it back in, deeper.

Gordan was humming. I felt the underside of his cock rubbing up and down across my hole. He was fully hard now, and seemed to be thoroughly enjoying himself.

"You might as well relax," he said. "This is not a short procedure. And we will continue until I come again. You may come as many times as you like in the interim."

The thin silver wand was twirled out of my urethra and he was reaching for a thicker, longer one. I moaned as it twirled inside me. Deeper inside me, before he extracted it an inch and twirled it in an inch and a quarter, extracted it an inch, and twirled it in an inch and a quarter. He revolved it slowly and I shuddered and moaned.

I could tell he was getting excited. He was humming louder and trembling and telling me how much he enjoyed this medical procedure and how much he could tell I was enjoying it. He wasn't letting me comment on that, but I had to admit that now that it was being done and I'd gotten over the initial shock of it, it wasn't half bad. I could feel myself building up cum.

When the third, larger rod was inserted, he let loose of my cock and moved his hand to my balls, which he gently kneaded, as I groaned and moved my hips slowly against his touch in an automatic rhythm of the fuck.

"You can come," he whispered. "It will just come up around the wand."

I turned my head to the side and stiffened, as a signal that I didn't want to do what he wanted me to do just because he wanted it.

But I felt the bulb of his cock at my hole then, and he was entering me again and slowly pushing to the depths. He twirled the thicker wand and slowly fucked my urethra channel with it while he was slow pumping my ass channel with his cock.

"Maybe you'll enjoy this," he said as he was extracting the sound wand. He held up a thin black tube with a bulb at the end of it. I watched in both horror and fascination as he fed the tube into my urethra. And then I threw my head back in a silent scream as I found out that when he squeezed the bulb on the end of the tube the tube inside me expanded and slowly deflated. Expand and deflate; expand and deflate, and my load burbled up the side of the tubing and out to slide down the sides of my cock. I collapsed back onto the table with a long, drawn-out moan.

"See, the coming was easy," he murmured as he slowly extracted the tubing.

I watched as his hand then wavered over the top of the cart and moved to a wand up the thickness and length gradation by several wands from the one he'd had in me last.

It looked like a telephone pole coming at my cock. It felt like a telephone pole as he slowly twirled it inside my urethra. I felt it go deeper inside than anything else he had stuck in there. I turned my head to the side, panting and trying to regularize my breathing, as he let loose of my cock, took my waist in his hands, and began to fuck me vigorously in earnest.

"The big finale," he cried out in a tortured, lust-filled voice.

I would have guessed that—at least I hoped so. He must be coming close to the end of the time he'd paid for. I certainly had to say he was getting his money's worth.

He had a hand gripping my balls again, stroking them, distending them, squeezing them rhythmically. I wondered if there had been a medical course in how to make a man come a second time in quick succession. If so, this doc had aced the course. He also had mastered the ability to come simultaneously, because as I

77

was shooting off again around the thick wand inside my urethra canal, I felt him filling the bulb of his condom inside me.

He leaned over me and released the ball gag, wanting to hear my "Oh fuckin' shit!" response as he pulled the telephone pole wand out of my cock.

I lay there panting hard still and moaning as he, with his cock still up my ass, lowered his chest on mine, and, for the first time, took my mouth in a deep kiss. I responded enough to let him know all was forgiven and that I wasn't going to tear him apart when he released me.

"You were magnificent," he whispered. "If I called again and asked for you by name, would you . . . ?"

"Yes," I murmured. "I have never before . . . and I've been around the block several times." I couldn't lie. It was one hot assignment. I wasn't wild about the shaving, but the sounding, which I'd only heard about before and had naturally shied away from, was way beyond hot when done right. And Gordan had really done it right.

He released me from the table and started talking about how good I was and how he was pleased with the service.

This was when the customer service I was known for and that brought me return requests kicked in. Unless the session was a real bust, I offered them a bit more off the clock. It made them feel twice the man and made them ask for me again and again. Comfortable now that nothing more threatening was going to happen, I turned to him and took his cheeks in my hands and gave him a big sloppy kiss on the lips. Our eyes were inches away from each other, and I watched him turn from surprise to pleased to renewed arousal.

"God, you're a superb cocksman," I whispered when we disengaged. "You used all the time on the clock. But, if you want, after we've built up again, you could fuck me again, if you want. Can even sound me with the wands again. I mean, please, when you feel like sounding someone again, I'm your man."

Flattered and delighted and immediately up to the challenge, he told me how much he'd like to do that in a flustered voice, and I turned and bent over onto the operating table on my now-hairless belly.

I felt the cool, wet lather at my asshole again, and then he was fucking me, slowly at first, and then in a frenzy, as I writhed under him and screamed out at the thick, deep taking. He covered my back with his torso and I turned my head and we kissed. He was trembling almost uncontrollably as he came again deep inside me.

He didn't pull out then, as I thought he might. He remained on top of me, pinning me to the table with his body. I felt his hands on my cock between my legs and then the coldness of the tip of a sounding wand at my piss slit. I cried out, "Oh, shit, oh fuck, Yes!" as I felt the wand twirl up into my urethra and one of his hands go to kneading my balls, coaxing yet another ejaculation from deep inside me.

I was whistling as I folded the extra thou into my billfold and settled into the BMW for the drive back down out of the Hollywood Hills. Leon wouldn't hear a whisper of complaint or description from me about this assignment. I knew that would drive him crazy.

And if Gordan asked for me again, and Leon made the assignment and imagined my consternation, the joke would be one him.

Roswell's Frontier Motel

Manuel held my hips steady as I shot off up into his face for a fourth rapid time, at last relieving that almost perpetual dull pain in my testicles, spent and no longer suffering, if at least for a few hours.

"Man, that's what I love about you," Manuel said, with a sly grin, as he licked my dick clean. "You come in buckets. It must be nice to be able to do that."

He turned me over on the bed in his El Paso apartment, straddled me, like a cowboy on his horse, and began stroking his luscious brown cock in and out of my ass.

"And this is what I love," I said between gasps. "But it's not fun, coming like that. I've got a condition—extra heavy cum production. I've got to have constant relief, or my balls drive me crazy with the pain. My girl at night, you most afternoons, and I've still got to go to the doctor every couple of weeks to be milked. In between I'm constantly pounding my own meat. I can't wait to outgrow this."

"Well, let me see about that," Manuel said, pulling me up on my knees while he continued to fuck into me hard. His hand came around and wrapped itself around my cock and milked me in rhythm with the stroking of his cock. In short order, I was gushing for him again.

"Ah, I see," he said. "You seem to be right."

Later, as we were engaging in postcoital fondling and kissing, he leaned over, opened the drawer to his bed stand, and took out a business card.

"Here," he said. "Try this place. Ask for the north wing."

I turned the card over and over in my hand, focusing on what was printed on it. It was for the Frontier Motel in Roswell, New Mexico, not all that far away from where I was temporarily working, in El Paso. I could get there on a Saturday and still be back at the defense lab by Monday morning.

"What happens there that would help my problem?" I asked.

"You'll have to go and see," Manuel said with a grin. "I've had others with your problem. I guess you could say I naturally sniff them out. And I've heard going to this place helps."

"Roswell, New Mexico," I pondered out loud. "Isn't that where they had those UFO sightings in the late 1940s that everyone talked and wrote so much about?"

"Yep," Manuel said. "The trip is worth it just for the tourism value. But you go to that motel and I think you'll get some relief from what you're calling a problem and I think I'd consider a gift."

Two weekends later, mid afternoon on a Saturday, I checked into the Frontier Motel in Roswell. The guy at the desk, who looked sort of creepy, gave me a sharp look when I asked for the north wing, but he didn't hesitate in fishing out a key and getting me registered. A studly looking black guy, all muscle and white teeth, had checked in right before I did, and when I pulled my car around to the somewhat isolated north wing, I saw that his Jeep Wrangler was parked near the door to the room I was given.

The north wing was sort of strange in appearance. There probably was only one hill of any height in Roswell, but the north wing of the Frontier Motel, a low, rambling series of wings around a swimming pool in the center court that obviously had been built at the beginning of the fifties or earlier, was built right up against that hill, its back wall abutting the hillside.

I hit the swimming pool right after I'd checked out the room. And the black guy, who apparently was on my wavelength, had done the same and was just settling on a lounger when I entered the pool area.

82

He said "Hi" to me in a pleasant enough way, but he had the same pained expression on his face that I got a couple of times a day. I quickly surmised that he had the same semen buildup problem I did, and I assumed that this was the secret of the motel's north wing. It was a place where guys with the same problem could come and engage in near-constant sex, and therefore help each other out. It seemed like not much of an answer to the problem, but it also probably was better than nothing. It certainly was better than what I was doing for the problem. It was getting hard to keep saying, "Hello, can we fuck for five straight hours and you let me come seven times, because, you know, I've got this problem?"

He could tell just by my walk and how I was delicately moving—and probably by that familiar expression on my face—that we shared this problem, and it wasn't long before we were back in my room and 69ing each other furiously.

He had a beautifully built chocolate body and a big black dick to die for. His balls were rock hard and ready to explode—constantly—just like mine were.

We were reversed on each other, sucking each other off, and coming again and again and again for more than two hours. Parting at last and laying there side by side, panting hard, we whispered a "thank-you" almost simultaneously. I didn't see this as a permanent solution as the guy in El Paso seemed to promise, but it was oh so good for now.

"Greatest relief I've had in months," I whispered.

"Me too," he responded. "Great body too. I'd like to do more. And I'm beginning to feel like I need it again."

"So soon? I think you may have it worse than I do."

"Do you take cock too?" he asked tentatively. "You've got a great ass. I'd love to split it, but . . ."

I turned toward him and placed a finger on his lips. "I'd love it. We're here for relief. If you're ready to fuck now, let's do it."

"I'll suck you off again first, though," he whispered.

I was laying back on the bed, my legs dangling off the side, and his mouth was playing my cock like it was a raspberry Popsicle. He had one hand pulling at my nipples and the fingers of the other one, heavily lubricated, were working my ass, preparing me for his own release.

He sucked me hard and relentlessly, and it wasn't long before my hands were bunching up wads of bedspread and my head was thrown back with my mouth open wide and howling at the ceiling as I came and came and came in big spoutings down his soft throat.

He swallowed me off in big gulps and then stood between my spread legs, gave me a grin and a chuckle, and just lifted my hips off the bed and pulled my ass onto his engorged cock. My torso was balanced on my shoulders and rising to meet his beefy midsection. I managed to get my legs up and running up his torso on either side of his head and held close to him by his ropy-muscled arms. He was pounding in me hard and deep, jabbering up a storm of appreciation at the tight ass I was entertaining him with and rocking my shoulders back and forth on the bed. I was talking back at him because I was equally impressed with the size and talent of his piece. I shot my load again.

He came too in floodings of cum and then pushed my body completely up on the bed, turned me on my stomach, and covered me with his body close. We explored each other where our hands could reach for a bit, but within fifteen minutes, I could feel both of us getting hard again, and my balls were telling me that I, at least, had another big load to give.

The black stud thrust his cock into my ass and pumped himself to another quick ejaculation and I gave the load I had to give to the bedspread my cock was being rubbed against in the rhythm of the black buck's fucking.

He came up off me then and we set a time to meet shortly after dinner to get our rocks off again—which is obviously what we both were there to do—and then he left me and I went into the shower.

I could have sworn as I was taking a piss before turning on the shower that I could hear soft, rather eerie music and the sounds of gentle moans coming from beyond the shower stall wall. This didn't really cut through my mellow feeling from the great fuck I'd gotten from the black stud at first. This was a motel, and the walls were bound to be thin, and there very well could just be a couple in the next room making whoopee to the radio. The black guy and I probably weren't the only ones here to take care of the same problem. But the shower was against the back wall, and that's where the sounds seemed to be coming from—and the back wall was against the hillside. There couldn't be another bank of rooms on that side of this wing.

Mellow I was, though, so I didn't give it much thought as I turned on the shower. And once the shower was on, I couldn't hear the noise at all.

I was soaped up real well and was rinsing off when the strangest things began happening. The water was getting thick and oily. It wasn't unpleasant, that oily feeling, cascading down my naked body and my tensing muscles and my still half-hard piece and my once-again heavy and hard—and beginning to pain me—balls. But it wasn't water, that was for sure. And there was a sensation of motion. My first thought was that we were having an earthquake. We were having an earthquake in the wilds of New Mexico, and here I was buck naked and oily in a shower stall and needing to ejaculate, as was so often the case with me—at least the ejaculate part.

But it was the shower stall that was moving. Just the shower stall. Nothing else in the bathroom was moving. The shower stall was turning. And as it turned, an opening was revealed in the back wall.

I tensed and, after I could catch up with my breath, I started screaming at what I saw beyond the opening. A large, dimly lit cavern. Moist walls, dripping water, a sense of a pulsating, dim light of changing colors, and soft music. But it was what was moving slowly around in the cavern that made me scream. Spider-like things. Living, moving spider-like things. Big ones. Each twice as tall as a man and four times as bulky. And, as my eyes adjusted to the light, I could see that there were men suspended under some of them, young, muscular naked men, loosely held close to the bellies of the spider-like creatures with strands of webbings. That was the moaning I had heard. The men were moaning.

I shrank back into the shower stall and turned to escape. But there was no escape. When the stall had turned, the back wall had cut off access to the bathroom—to the world that made sense and wasn't terrifying. The only opening now was into the cavern.

85

Still, I shrank back as far as I could against the wall. But I was oily now and slid down into a fetal position on the floor of the stall.

Tentacle like things—a giant spider-like being's appendages—were coming into the stall and wrapping themselves around me. I screamed again as they drew me out of the stall and into the cavern beyond. I watched in panic as the wall of the shower stall turned again and then I was trapped in the cavern with these . . . whatever these were. I found myself placed on my back on some sort of table or stone altar. Beside me was another table. On top of it was a graduated series of silver rods. I moaned, my memory going back to having watched videos where those rods were used by men in an extra extreme sex act called sounding. The spider-like being that was imprisoning me had me held by claws on the end of four of its appendages, one each on arms and legs pulled down off the side of the table I was laying on. The body of the spider was hovering over me. A cock-like appendage jutting out of its belly forced itself inside my mouth, filling my cavity so that I couldn't talk or scream.

I could still see down the length of my body, though. An appendage of the spider held my cock upright and another one reached over and selected one of the thinner silver rods from the side table. I tried to arch my back in a silent scream, but the spider was holding me perfectly still. The creature then proceeding to do just what I'd seen in the videos on sounding. It slowly twirled the rod into my piss slit. It moved the rod up and down when it was a few inches inside and I came in flow of cum around the sides of the sounding wand. The spider made a humming sound and two more spiders came over and hummed as well. My sense was that they were excited and pleased about something that had happened. I came, not being able to help it, but also in waves and waves of pleasurable ecstasy at this extreme form of fucking I'd never experienced before, each successive time my penis was fucked this way by the spider alien with ever thicker and longer rods.

My penis was invaded by increasingly thicker wands, and as soon as a wand was buried deep and the creature stroked it up and down inside my urethra canal, I came again. Each time I ejaculated the spiders gathered around me and hummed excitedly. It then became obvious that this had been some sort of test—and that I had passed. They had wanted me to reload quickly and come again and again.

The spider alien gathered me up and I saw that I was being moved toward an area where other men were suspended under the bellies of aliens and were moaning. The spider brought me under the belly of one of the beings, which wasn't linked to a man and which was sighing quietly. The delivering creature turning me so I was stretched out and my chest was turned toward what must be the chest of the being. I looked down, between my legs, as the appendages pulled my legs up to its sides and tucked my feet and calves into some sort of pocket sack on either of its side, holding them there close and opening my legs wide, letting me feel that there was something beating away inside that spider-like thorax, a heart of some sort. When I looked down, I saw that there was a long, thick thing looking very much like an elephant-hung cock hanging between the being's last set of appendages. The cock-like thing was all nubby and it had a mushroom cap with a whip-like device hanging out of its head. Looking up, I saw another cock-like proboscis hanging out of the being's round little head—and from its belly at the level of my navel was a smaller cock-like proboscis and at chest level two smaller appendages with small suction cup-like hands on them.

Spent from screaming and completely terrorized, I was moaning now. But it wasn't moaning like the other imprisoned men around me were doing. Their moaning was that of passion and satisfied lust.

Why were my feelings different? Why weren't they as terrified as I was?

The spider-like being was lowering its head at me. All I could focus on, though, was that black cock-like thing swinging down from where its nose should be. The tip of it was at my lips, and I compressed them, trying to keep the invader out. But it was forcing my lips open and entering me. It was swabbing the inside of my cheeks with its mushroom cap and secreting a not-unpleasant oily substance into my mouth. A substance that had a calming influence on me as it trickled down my throat. The probe was also moving around in my mouth, caressing my inner cheeks and making small rhythmic movements toward the back of my throat.

I was being face fucked by the spider's head proboscis, but increasingly I didn't care. The soft, eerie music was building and flowing into my senses, and the moaning from those other men around me—moaning punctuated frequently with a cry of overflowing passion and ejaculation—was becoming more prominent and was beckoning to me.

The two suction cup-like hands were sucking on my nipples, and I felt the bulbous mushroom cap of the spider's other cock, the long, thick, dangling one, caressing the rim of my oiled asshole.

I lurched and tried to turn from it as it slowly rotated and screwed into me, reaching a depth that no human man had explored. But the spider had a firm hold on me with its various appendages, webbing, and the sheathing of my feet and calves at its sides. Suction cup-crowned appendages I hadn't seen before applied themselves to my balls and worked them, teasing testicles into semen production that needed no teasing. Something inside the spider enveloped my toes and began sucking them sensuously. The muscles of my feet and calves were being massaged. Appendages were massaging my butt cheeks and spreading them wider, as the spider's cock probe dug deeper up my ass channel and thickened. My whole body was rhythmically being moved back and forth on the cock deep inside me, and the beating of the creature's heart was being calibrated to my own. I was part of the creature now. The cock probe's nobby sides were undulating along my tender passage walls and stroking my prostate and that whip-like device on the head giving tingles of sensations on walls not yet being discovered, stretched, and massaged.

My cock was going to full attention and I managed to cast my gaze down the length of my torso just well enough to see the spider's probe at my navel level whirring and emitting a thinnish hollow tube about a third of an inch wide. The probe moved around until it felt the cap of my erect and throbbing cock. Then as I watched in what should have been horror, but, thanks to the calming mouth swabbing, was more curiosity, leathery prongs sprang out from the side of the probe and attached themselves to the cap of my cock, holding it in place as more of the tube glided out of the spider's probe and into my piss slit. It widened as it ran into me and I moaned to this kind of fucking that was so similar to the sounding I had already succumbed to.

I held very still now, know how sensitive this invasion was, as the tube ran down a good distance into my urethra.

I could see as I looked closer that there was a line running out of the base of this probe and up toward the ceiling of the cavern, where there was a transparent container of some sort, into which whitish fluid was running in spurts from other lines running up from the bellies of the other spiders that were slowly sliding around the room.

I wasn't being penis fucked; I was being milked for my cum.

This also was when I saw the black stud. He was under the belly of the nearest spider to me. And he was as attached as I was. And he was moaning for the spider in a way he hadn't moaned for me.

We were all being milked. It was all being collected in that container up there. For what purpose I could only surmise.

But I wasn't much interested in surmising just now. The probes invading my body were working in unison. They were gently moving in and out of me, coming close to the entrance of their assigned orifice and then invading a bit deeper with each reentry. I was being fucked three ways at once and having my nipples and testicles worked to boot. And it was like no other sensation I'd ever had before. The being had left my hands free, and I wrapped them around my cock and gently pumped myself in countermovement to the stroking of the tube running inside my tool, helping to bring myself to an orgasm like I'd never known. And then another one and another one. I no longer felt the tightness and ache of needing to ejaculate. I was being milked down to the level of a mix of comfort, satisfaction, and sexual pleasure.

Again and again I came—and prodigiously and with a great cry of release—and I watched a stream of whitish fluid run up through the tubing coming out of my piss slit and on up the lines toward the container above.

I raised my hands to the silky softness, yet rock hard, body of the creature cradling my body. As I ran hands along the surface, I found knobs that must have been nipples, because when I rubbed them, the creature moaned and sighed and pulled me deeper onto its cock inside my ass canal, pulling me faster and harder on the cock as I rubbed and pinched its nipples and cried out in ecstasy at the deeper, more vigorous fuck.

As I ejaculated again, the creature do so inside my channel as well, and I could feel the warm fluid flow down the side of its cock and out my hole. Other creatures gathered around mine and babbled to each other excitedly, which led me to believe that it was relatively rare for one of the creatures to be moved to ejaculate. I felt an increased sense of well-being flow over me at our mutual orgasms. I truly felt as one with the creature now, feeling that we were working together toward some worthy goal.

The spider gave a little sigh, and its heart beat a bit faster as I continued to ejaculate for it, and I could almost believe that the fuck was as sensual for it as it was for me. The soft music and the moaning around me increased its volume in my brain as the various appendages on the spider caressed my body, encouraging me to reload. And reload I did, and soon the sensuous moaning I heard was my own, and I was making another flooding deposit in the large jar at the ceiling. The creature ejaculated again, apparently getting the hang of us firing off together.

A sixth time, a ninth time, the dozenth time—both of us shooting off together. I had never felt as pleasantly spent and thankfully drained before. More coaxing and a thirteenth time. The spider was trembling with pleasure. I was a star producer. And the gathering of other, excited creatures about mine indicated that mine was a star performer as well.

And then I woke . . . naked . . . under the running water of the shower stall in the north wing room of the Frontier Motel in Roswell, New Mexico. It was daylight.

I didn't for a second think that this had been a dream. I felt great. My balls didn't ache. There was no semen buildup. At daylight there always had been semen buildup and jacking off had always been my first chore of the day.

I dried and dressed and went to the motel's reception desk.

"Was there something wrong with your room?" the creepy desk clerk asked. And he looked like he was prepared for some weird song and dance.

"Not at all," I answered. "In fact, if the room's available, I want to book it for tonight too."

That afternoon, I saw the big black stud at the pool again. And although we were pleasant to each other and exchanged knowing smiles, there was no offer of a relief fuck from either of us today. He confirmed that, like me, he was extending his stay. And we were both saving ourselves for that night.

Do You Trust Me?

Angelo had been so tense through his set at the café this evening that he was afraid the tension could be heard in his voice or in a change in how he coaxed the music out of the strings of his guitar. But those who were here most every night, sitting around smoking and drinking long after the food service had been shut down, didn't seem to have reacted any differently than usual. Although all of the regulars in the café were encouraging and always bantered with Angelo in a way that showed him he was liked and at home in the seaside Italian village of Positano, where he'd been born and raised, they had come to receive his musical sets in the café in the evening as a given that was just part of the atmosphere of the place. Only the tourists paid close attention to his performances.

Angelo didn't mind. He was doing this mostly because he liked it, although the little bit that the café owner, Maria, paid him plus the occasional tip from a tourist were welcome supplements to his income. Angelo was a fisherman, sailing out alone in his small boat six mornings a week, casting his net, and, by twilight bringing his catch, meager as it usually was, to the fish markets on the pier in the small harbor of Positano. This picturesque village closely climbed from the Mediterranean up the steep slopes the surrounding mountains that paralleled Italy's eastern coast, west along a rugged coastline from Salerno.

And this was, Angelo believed, all just temporary for him, including the fishing with the boat he had inherited from his father, who had inherited it from his own father. Angelo would be going to America at the first opportunity—to maybe be in the movies. That was his dream. And Angelo was a dreamer.

And not just a dreamer. Angelo was also seen as a dream by the women of Positano and by not a few men of the village as well. He had dark, sultry, movie star looks. And perhaps that was what had set off his dream of going to America. For as long as he could remember, people were telling him that, with his looks, he should be in Hollywood—or at least in Rome.

What had suddenly made Angelo tense in playing his café set and had upset his world was Guido, another young fisherman who had been in playful competition with Angelo in casting the nets off the Positano shore for a couple of years. Guido was sitting at the bar, nursing as few drinks as possible for Maria to let him occupy a barstool and smoke cigarette after cigarette, as he had done nearly every evening that Angelo had played. Guido was also dark and sultry, and very well put together. He just was two steps behind Angelo in every department of desirability and had known he was since the two were boys—both that he was that well put together and that he wasn't quite as put together well as Angelo was. Hence—at least Angelo had thought—the friendly competition and why Guido always seemed to be there, somewhere, in the background wherever Angelo was. Of course Positano was not a large town, so—other than the looks of want, combined with envy, Guido gave Angelo—there wasn't much to be remarked that they were always somewhere in proximity of one another.

It had been what Guido had asked Angelo to do the evening before, after Angelo had finished his set, that had changed Angelo's world, made him nervous in the close-scrutiny nearness of Guido, and made Angelo rethink why Guido was always hovering around.

Guido had asked—no begged—Angelo to fuck him, saying that he had wanted this ever since the two were in school together.

Angelo hadn't, in a million years, caught Guido's attention to him as signaling any such desire.

94

He had refused, of course, as gently as he could. He had told Guido that there was no chance that he could be a friend to Guido in that way. What he didn't tell Guido was why. Guido had made it quite clear that he wanted Angelo inside him. But to the extent that Angelo had ever thought of having sex with another man—which had, in fact, crossed his mind, sometimes in ways that disturbed him and had, thus far, caused him to hold himself above having sex with anyone, man or woman—those thoughts had seen him in the same position of need and want as Guido had declared he suffered and wanted Angelo to deliver him from. If Angelo was ever to have sex with a man, he wanted the other man inside him.

But Guido, although he had done no more than to show and express regret, had not taken Angelo's answer as a "forever no." He had simply asked Angelo to think about it. And here he was, tonight, sitting in his customary place at the bar, fully attentive to and ever smiling upon Angelo. The difference now was that Angelo knew what Guido wanted—and it wasn't just the continuance of a friendship of two young men who had grown up together in a small seaside town and who both went to sea as fishermen in boats handed down to them by their fathers and their fathers' fathers.

Guido's attentive smile now bored into Angelo as he played. And it wasn't just Guido this evening. Often tourists came in to the café, having heard him play his guitar and sing, and sat watching him. A good many of them would want to watch Angelo even if he didn't do anything but exist as the beauty in form that he was. To tourists, he was all that was sensual Italian beauty and allure.

And sometimes the foreign residents of the town—people who weren't passing tourists and may even have been Italians living here for decades but who were still considered foreign visitors in one way or another because they hadn't been born and raised in Positano—came to the café, having heard about Angelo and both his beauty and his music. Some of the wealthiest people in the town—who were treated with distant respect because of the revenue they brought to the region—were actually foreigners. There was a whole enclave of them to the south of the town, living in villas along the coast and beyond the mountain spur that went down to the sea there and defined the edge of the town. Villas were strung along the coast to the south, perched on the rocky slopes of the mountains and with steps down to small, private beaches below, each separated from the neighboring villa by rock formations tumbling down to the sea.

It was off these beaches that Angelo did most of his fishing, both because the fish ran well there and because Angelo enjoyed watching the activity in the villas of the rich foreigners through his binoculars. And some of the foreigners, aware of Angelo's frequent fishing visits off their coast also watched him move, in his skimpy loincloth bathing suit around his fishing vessel.

Angelo liked to watch the coastline because often the villa owners and their young guests came down to their private beaches in the nude. And sometimes they fucked on the beach. Angelo enjoyed watching this, no matter what the mix was in the coupling of the sexes.

That's why Angelo knew who the two men at the table were who were scrutinizing him as closely as Guido was—and who were causing him as much embarrassment. The older man owned one of the largest villas perched above the sea, one with extensive verandas and frequently with young, very good looking and well-muscled men roaming around in very little. Angelo already knew the older man to be Doran Kokinos, a grossly wealthy Greek shipping magnate, who spent several months a year in his Positano coast villa. The man was in his late fifties at least and, though solidly built and well-muscled, was squat and a bit rotund and extremely hirsute with salt-and-pepper hair. His features all were thickish and slightly piggish, and he glowered more than looked, under bushy eyebrows, at whatever caught his attention. But he had impeccable taste in young men, and he fucked them well on the beach.

Angelo knew Kokinos fucked men—and young men— because Angelo had, through his binoculars, spied him doing so from time to time on his terraces or down on the beach. And Angelo's binoculars were high powered enough for Angelo to know that what Kokinos lacked in body beauty, he made up for in cock girth and length.

Kokinos had been in the café for hours this evening, the first time Angelo had known him to be there, and his glower had been trained on Angelo, piercing his composure during both of Angelo's musical sets. What occurred to Angelo, though, and that had deepened his embarrassment and apprehension, was that perhaps this wasn't the first visit of Doran Kokinos to the café. Perhaps he had been here before and perhaps before he had trained his attention on Angelo just as he had done this evening— and Angelo, in his innocence, had just not caught what was in the air. Perhaps the single, simple declaration by Guido the previous evening had awakened Angelo to a reality that had, in his innocence, not been part of his real world before—but inevitably was part of that world now.

And when Angelo thought upon that, the image of that cock of Kokinos's sinking in and withdrawing from and then sinking again into the ass of the young prey of the day on the beach below his villa gave Angelo a chill of envy. The man's ugliness in other ways seemed only to add to the mystery and fantasy of Angelo's sexual longings.

To his added embarrassment, Angelo, in turn, had had to struggle not to give his undivided attention this evening to Kokinos's table companion. The man was younger than Kokinos—by far—but older than Angelo's own barely twenty years. The man struck Angelo as an American—a blond, athletic American. Perhaps it was the apparent openness of him and the ready smile. Whatever it was, he had charisma and an assurance about himself that was justified by his rugged good looks. Now there, Angelo had thought, when he first noticed the young man—noticed him noticing Angelo—is a true Hollywood movie star type.

Angelo couldn't remember having ever seen that young man with his binoculars, and that thought had set off another thought. He wondered what the man looked like in the altogether or in a skimpy Speedo. It was a thought that had made Angelo forget what song he was singing at the time and made him stop, apologize, blame it on being thirsty, taken a swig of his water, and then start on a song that may have been the same one, but again may not have been, for all the attention he was giving it.

Angelo was distressed at the longings that Guido had loosed in him the previous day by openly talking of sex between men. Angelo had mostly been able to suppress his thinking—at least consciously—of these things to this point. Guido had unleashed that monster from the cave Angelo had locked it in.

In that patron-, raucous discussion-, and smoke-filled café room, with patrons tumbling out onto the tables set up at the edge of the narrow, cobblestoned, winding street, Angelo had struggled through two sets feeling that he was pinned to the wall by three sets of eyes—Guido's, Doran Kokinos's, and the mysterious, mesmerizing blond's. This was the first time he'd ever felt like this. And, in his imagination, Angelo was lying under each of the men, his hips rotating, and something throbbing and thrusting, stretching his insides.

And it was all Guido's fault.

Forcing himself not to look at any of the three when his set was over, Angelo put his guitar in the stand next to his stool, where it would still be the next time he came to the café to play and sing, and turned to go through the door behind him covered by a beaded curtain that led through a corridor to the kitchen on one side, bathrooms on the other, a storeroom and Maria's office and then to an exit that hovered ten feet above the street below the one the café was located on. Descending the rickety wooden staircase there would put Angelo just one street above his own, where he had two rooms and a kitchenette and bathroom at the top of the building he had inherited and where the rent from the two floors below his made his life as comfortable as most any other resident of Positano.

He was just beyond the doors to the restrooms, however, when Guido caught up to him, swung him around and pinned his back to the wall with his body. Guido was slightly taller and heavier than Angelo, and he was just as strong. Caught by surprise, Angelo was slow to react with any sense of defensiveness.

"Please, Angelo. Take me to your rooms. Or come with me to mine. I can't deny my want for you any longer."

"Guido, no. I can't. I told you yester—"

Angelo wasn't able to finish the sentence, as Guido was pressing at his lips with his own and crushing him against the wall. One of Guido's hands was pressing on Angelo's crotch.

Caught completely by surprise, Angelo was slow to react. He was looking around wildly, not knowing why he was here like this, why Guido was in such a frenzy, or what he should do next. His eyes caught the movement of the beaded curtain separating the back corridor from the main café room, and he saw movement there. A man. The blond man Angelo thought of as the suave American.

The expression on the American's face was one of surprise. But then it turned to an amused smile, and, rather than withdrawing, the man stood there, watching.

Adrenalin finally surged through Angelo's body, and he broke away from Guido with a, "We can't . . . I can't . . . sorry," and he rushed through the door at the end of the corridor and almost lost his footing on the precarious wooden steps of the staircase down to the lower street.

Once in his room, he turned off his lights and moved out onto the small terrace he had that overlooked the Mediterranean and the lower town as it cascaded down to the harbor. He stood, watching the moonlight on the sea for several moments, trembling and overwhelmed by the strange, unfamiliar sensations accosting him. He was surprised—and embarrassed—to realize that he was hard.

He stripped off his trousers, briefs, and T-shirt and laid down on the chaise lounge on the terrace, and, as he looked up at the bright constellations in the clear night sky, he began to masturbate. What was this terrible—but perhaps glorious—monster that Guido had awakened in him? He had no idea, and his emotions were conflicted. As he slowly and rhythmically beat himself off, though, he realized that an image of a man was floating in his brain and feeding his arousal. It wasn't Guido, though. It was the image of that smiling all-American blond, standing, naked, in the doorway at the café, the beads of the curtain caressing his body, as he watched Angelo masturbating—and stroked his own hard cock with a loose fist.

A second image swam up. An ugly face and a squat but solid body. And much black curly hair. But an air of authority—

and a bit of cruelty—and an invading monstrous cock that had Angelo panting and whimpering of how filling it was. As the mastering cock in Angelo's fantasy began to pump his channel, he threw his head back, ejaculated onto his stomach, and muttered the name Doran Kokinos.

Instead of giving him the lift he expected, these fantasies brought a sourness to Angelo's mood. This was wrong. He wanted to think of lying under a beautiful man like the blond American or even Guido—before Guido had burst that bubble and revealed himself as a receiver rather than a driver—not one who was old and ugly such as Kokinos. Did the aura of authority or the size of the cock really make that much difference? And, even if the cock was all important, he had not seen what the blond American had to offer.

* * * *

"Are you just going to leave me down here, or will you give me a hand up?"

Angelo looked around in shock, not seeing where the voice was coming from, completely nonplused to hear a voice at all. He was on his fishing boat, all alone, or so he thought, off the beaches below the villas of the rich foreigners strung along the Amalfi coast south of Positano.

He had set his nets and then gone to the stern of the boat with his binoculars and scanned the beaches and the villas perched on the side of the mountains above as he liked to do. He told himself that he hadn't stationed the boat off from Doran Kokinos's villa on purpose, but, of course, he had. And in doing so, he had been rewarded.

Not long after taking up his station, he had seen activity on one of the villa's terraces and then the figure of a tall, well-built—and very well-equipped, he could see, because the man was naked—young man descending the stone steps between the villa and the beach. He had a beach towel over one arm and a canvas bag slung over his shoulder.

To Angelo's great interest, the young man engaged in a few aerobic exercises while standing next to the towel that he had unfurled on the beach in front of a sky-blue cabana tent.

After a few moments of surreptitious work with the binoculars, Angelo ascertained that it was the same blond man Angelo had seen at the café, sitting with Doran Kokinos, the previous evening.

Angelo laid down flat on his belly at the stern of the boat, with just the lens of the binoculars showing above the gunwales and watched the blond, who he thought of as "the American," do his calisthenics. The rough wood of the boat hull punished Angelo's bare chest, but unheeding of that, he unbuttoned the fly of his skimpy shorts, pulled out his hardening cock, encircled the staff with the hand that wasn't holding the binoculars, and moved his hips, letting the head of his cock rub through his cupped palm and across the pile of netting in the bottom of the boat.

When the blond man turned and went into the cabana tent, Angelo realized that he should have pulled his nets in some time ago to see if he'd caught any fish and then set them again. It took him nearly half an hour to do that, and he had just finished when he heard the voice.

"I say, you going to leave me just hanging onto the side?"

Angelo raced back to the stern of the boat. Two well-muscled, lightly tanned arms, emerging from the water next to the boat, were slung over the gunwales. He grabbed for the arms and helped the blond American climb on board the boat. He was naked and wet, but he had the canvas bag slung over his back by a string around his neck.

Both the surprise of his arrival and the beauty of his body took Angelo's breath away.

"You wouldn't happen to have a dry towel, would you?" he asked in broken Italian.

"Yes. Yes, I have. Just uno minute," Angelo stammered.

"You speak English," the blond said, sounding quite relieved.

"I take in school. I go to America some day and I want to speak good American. You American?" he asked shyly.

"Yes, I'm American. And I'm shuddering from the cold water at the moment. It's a longer swim than I anticipated."

"Uh," Angelo muttered, still dumbfounded by the man's appearance and by the casual, comfortable attitude he was taking despite his nudity.

"The towel? You were going to find me a towel?"

"Yes, of course," Angelo stammered, as he backpedaled toward the small cabin at the center of the boat.

When he came back, the American was still standing there, in a provocative pose, but he'd opened the canvas bag and extracted a bottle of liquor and a couple of plastic glasses. "I hope you don't mind Johnny Walker Red. It was the most ready at hand in Dodo's bar."

"Dodo?"

"Doran Kokinos. I believe you saw us at the café last night. He was very impressed with you. In fact, he'd like to meet you. I call him Dodo. For some reason he prefers that. He's Greek, you know. He probably doesn't know the connotation of that in the States. It does seem to suit him. But here I am, running on, and you're probably very thirsty from all of the fishing work you've been doing—not to mention the work with the binoculars."

Angelo had barely been able to keep up with what the American had been saying. He had no trouble understanding the part about binoculars, though, and he blushed from the realization he'd been caught as a voyeur. And he was even more nonplused to see that the American was hard and not seeming to be the least self-conscious about it.

And, yes, he knew Johnny Walker well, although he'd rarely been able to cadge more than a couple of shots of it at a time himself. The foreigners had it shipped in by the case during the Christmas season and handed bottles of it out as gratuities for those in the village who had supported their lifestyle with goods and services throughout the year. For two weeks after Christmas, Johnny Walker red became the gold standard of Positano and was filtered down in smaller, recycled bottles throughout the fabric of the town—to when it was all gone until the next year. Angelo rarely got more than two shots of it himself in a year. And here the American—the beautifully built and handsome American of the open, broad smile—was offering to share an entire bottle with him.

"So, shall we drink and share sea stories?"

"Yes, if you wish," Angelo said shyly, trying not to look at the American's magnificent cock, but not being able to take his eyes away.

"Good. We talk and become better acquainted. I know that your name is Angelo. Mine is Brett. We drink . . . and talk . . . and then we fuck. But we won't do much of the first two before getting around to the fucking, I hope, because, as you can see I'm ready for that." He moved his hips back and forth, sending his hard cock shimmying for Angelo to take full note of.

Angelo did a double-take and his jaw dropped to his chest. But the American did not seem to notice or skip a beat.

"I'll fuck you, if you don't mind—unless you insist otherwise. Then we can go up to the house and you can meet Doran. He wants to fuck you too. Anyone ever tell you that you had a friggin' beautiful body and smile? You could be in movies."

"I'm . . . I'm sorry. I can't. I don't . . . I never. I will take you back to the beach in my small boat." Angelo had turned red in a blush and, without effort, taken on a crestfallen look that the American, Brett, couldn't help but understand as genuine surprise, consternation—and regret.

It was, perhaps the note of regret that helped Brett to brazen it through. "Sorry, dude, my mistake. I assumed when I saw you making out with the other guy last night—"

"We . . . weren't, how you put it, making out. Guido wants something I can't give him. It was nothing. You just saw a minute of mistake. Sorry. I take you back to the beach."

"No, I'm the one who is sorry. But you can't blame me for trying, and you looked like you were interested enough. And I say we don't burden your small boat with this bottle of Johnny Walker. Let's go ahead and polish it off as long as we're here. What do you say? And about that chap last night. You can't give him what he wants because he wants to be fucked? You know what that should mean to me, don't you?"

"You are confusing me. I don't know what it should mean."

"Well, then, let's back up a bit. Would you like to help me with this bottle of Johnny Walker or not?"

"Well . . . OK."

* * * *

"Do you trust me?" It came in a whisper, but it shot through Angelo's brain like an electric jolt. "Trust me to treat you right. Let me fuck you. I'll make you love it. My cock is aching to be inside you." The strike of awakening from the follow-up phrases were even stronger than the nudge and questioning of Angelo's trust.

The empty liquor bottle was knocking around in the stern of the boat, slipping from one side to the other as the waves gently rocked the boat. The two plastic glasses were closer to hand in the bow where the two men were stretched out against each other on a pile of netting. The glasses made more of a clunking sound as they rolled against the gunwales.

The bottle had been three-quarters empty, with Angelo doing most of the drinking, before Brett had put an arm around the young Italian's shoulders and pulled him in close. Angelo couldn't remember—or say—when or why he had let the American kiss him. All he could have said was that it was both sweet and hot in comparison to the kiss Guido had stolen from him the previous evening.

After that first kiss, Angelo lost count and hardly even noticed when Brett had moved a hand into the unbuttoned fly of the shorts that Angelo had unbuttoned himself some time earlier when he was watching the American on the beach with the binoculars—and forgotten to do up again.

Angelo had whimpered something about it being wrong and that he didn't do such things—had never done them before— when Brett had taken possession of his embarrassingly hard cock and had mentioned something about trust that first time.

"But you're not saying that you don't want to do them," Brett had countered in a matter-of-fact voice. "I think you do want me to fuck you." Angelo had said nothing to this.

The American had urged the last of the bottle of Johnny Walker on Angelo and then had taken the young Italian to heaven with a slow hand job that Angelo had objected to with his voice— but only with his voice. His hips had a mind of their own and it wasn't long until, with a low laugh, the American loosened his grip

104

on the cock, and Angelo moved his hips, fucking himself to ejaculation in the encasing hand.

The bottle finished, and Angelo panting and whimpering, putting up some semblance of a struggle that was a stronger one in his mind than in reality, Brett had lowered himself to stretch on the netting in the bow of the boat and brought Angelo down to cuddle on top of him with the young man's shoulder blades against Brett's chest.

Angelo's visual world was revolving in a motion that went with the gentle swaying of the boat, his ears were ringing, his thoughts were sluggish in forming, and he was moaning quietly as Brett's hands roamed over his body.

"Trust me. I will be good to you. God, you have a beautiful body," Brett was murmuring.

Angelo could feel the man's insistent hard cock rubbing up the small of his back.

"Let me inside you. I will fuck you to heaven."

The American's hands had moved to the waistline of Angelo's shorts, which, miraculously, still rode his hips. He pushed the shorts down a bit, and Angelo objected weakly. A hand went under the waist of the shorts and along the curve of Angelo's butt cheek, moving toward, and then to, the rim of his entrance.

"You say you've never been fucked before? Yes, it feels tight. But it will open for me. I will do you right."

Angelo moaned and reached around and grabbed the American's hand through the thin material of his shorts. Not even he was sure if he had done so to try to force the hand away or to hold it there.

But then, again with a low laugh, the American was pushing Angelo's shorts down off his hips.

"Do you trust me? Trust me to treat you right. Let me fuck you. Roll onto your stomach. Let's get these shorts off. I'm going to fuck you. You want it."

Gathering all of his strength, Angelo pulled himself out of the American's embrace and went, first, up on his knees. And then up into a crouch. He looked down into the face of the American with an expression of torment and consternation. "Sorry. I can't . . . I don't . . . Just sorry. It is too much."

Brett turned on his back and locked his fists behind his head, stretching out to put his musculature at its most compelling. His hard cock stood straight up from his neatly trimmed groin. A beatific smile was planted across his face. If he was angry or frustrated, it didn't show. He yawned to show Angelo that there was nothing serious going on.

"Well, if you can't you can't. But I gave you a hand job. Perhaps you could return the favor?"

Angelo's expression was one of regret and instead of kneeling back down, he stood up and backed up a step toward the door into the cabin. "It isn't right . . . this isn't me. But I thank you for the Johnny Walker."

"I think it is you, dear boy," Brett answered. "Although," he followed with a sigh, "Perhaps it isn't you on this particular day. Too bad about the hand job, though. It could have moved on to something wonderful." He moved to stand up, and as he did so, Angelo retreated to the cabin doorway.

"Give me a minute and I'll take you back to the beach in the small boat," he said, and then he pulled himself into the cabin. There wasn't anything he really had to do in there; he just needed to be separated from the temptation long enough to gather his wits and his resolve.

The realization that the man really did intend to put his cock inside him had pulled Angelo out of the drunken stupor— but only enough for him to realize that he was no match for the charm, assurance, and power of the American. He didn't know what he'd say or do when he came out of the cabin. Chances were good, he knew, that he would lay down on the netting and open his legs to the American. All he knew was that he couldn't stay in the cabin; he had to go out on deck.

But if he went back out on deck it would be admitting that he wanted the American to fuck him. It was all so confusing. Why couldn't he admit to what he knew he wanted to do?

He went back out on deck. The American was gone. Angelo went to the bow of the boat and could see the bobbing head of the man as he swam his way back toward the beach.

With mixed feelings, Angelo quickly took in his nets and dumped the wriggling fish down into the hold of the boat. Then he took the boat out to sea—not north toward Positano, but directly out to sea to where he knew he'd be alone.

He was hard and throbbing throughout this time, and when he was safely away from the land, he stripped off his shorts, stretched out on the netting at the bow, made an opening down through the netting for his dick to slide into, and fucked the netting to his relief, all the time imagining what the gorgeous American hunk could have done with him.

* * * *

Angelo remained on the boat that night, bobbing back and forth out at the edge of the Positano harbor. His face was turned to the lights of the town, climbing the ring of mountains surrounding it on the three sides not taken by the waters of the harbor, without being aware of the beauty of the setting. He was scrunched down in the stern of the boat, resting on a netting coil, almost in a fetal position, and trying to make sense of his life and, more important, of his desires and what, essentially, he was.

He still hadn't decided what he wanted out of life—or rather he had, and the prospect of it frightened him—when the rays of the sun were beginning to lighten the sky to the west, behind the mountaintops. Almost on autopilot, though, he began to prepare for the needs of the day. He motored back into the pier only long enough to offload his scanty catch from the interrupted previous day and then he was chugging back out of the harbor. He turned the boat north this morning, not wanting to be seen again—at least so soon—off the villas to the south. He told himself that it was because he never intended to go there again, but, in reality, he just didn't want to exhibit eagerness for what he had rejected the previous day.

As the boat slowly cut through the waves, he checked his nets for rips, grabbed a bite to eat from what he had gotten at a food stall when he'd offloaded the previous day's catch, and turned his face north. He knew it would be a short fishing day, because he was near exhaustion and had two sets to play at the café that evening. He would need to be back by early afternoon so that he could clean himself and catch a few hours of sleep before nightfall.

Angelo had trouble sleeping that afternoon, even though he was dog tired. He couldn't help thinking about the blond American, Brett—and wondering—no, hoping, if he was honest—that the man would be at the café that evening. If he was there alone, without the older man, Doran Kokinos, maybe Angelo would try to talk with him, would maybe tease him a bit, make him think that Angelo would go with him and then back off. But then maybe changing his mind and doing what he knew he wanted to do. He would do nothing if the Greek was there, though. He scared Angelo more than a bit, especially because Angelo was attracted to him too, but in a different way, in a way that Angelo knew if he went with the ugly Greek, there was no limit to what Angelo would be willing to do for another man. The American had been so forward the previous day, and, in hindsight, Angelo knew exactly what the liquor was for—and what it had caused. The American was so casual and nonchalant about the whole thing. Taking Angelo for granted and thereby showing a lot of conceit. Angelo thought he might get a bit of his own back, do a little bit of teasing, and when the American's tongue was hanging out, just walk off.

Then maybe they'd be on equal ground and could start anew. Then maybe Angelo would be ready to take the plunge. Or could consider again doing so.

The American indeed was there when Angelo arrived at the café just before he was scheduled to go on for his first set. And the older Greek man wasn't there. But Guido was. The American, Brett, and Guido were at the same table the American and the Greek had been at a couple of evenings before. And Guido looked oh so proud of himself. Just like he'd already gotten the satisfaction from someone else that he had begged from Angelo and not gotten.

This didn't exactly make Angelo feel relieved. He tried to remember if he'd seen Guido out in his fishing boat that day. But he couldn't remember seeing the boat in the harbor, and Guido always went south to do his fishing. Angelo almost always went south too, but today he'd gone north, so it wasn't unusual that he couldn't remember having seen Guido out in his boat.

They weren't touching or anything when Angelo first saw them, and the American had his eyes on Angelo during the whole set, but Guido had changed. He now had his eyes on the American rather than on Angelo. And Angelo couldn't really tell by the end of the set that no touching was going on. The American kept his hands above the table, but Angelo couldn't have sworn that Guido hadn't put his hands on the American's forearm or thigh a time or two while Angelo sang. Guido's submissiveness and the American's possession of him were obvious.

The American had already covered Guido with his body and fucked him. Angelo was sure of that, and the knowledge disturbed him, even though he knew it shouldn't have.

Angelo had to take a piss after his first set. He was only gone briefly, having intended to watch the pair from behind the beaded curtain separating the back rooms from the main one before his next set began. But the two were gone when Angelo came back to do his second set.

He knew he didn't play and sing too well for the second set. He was stewing over what he was missing out on—and that perhaps Guido was not—and still arguing with himself over what he wanted.

He must not have done too badly in the set and must have conveyed his sense of both melancholy and sensuality, because a tourist followed him out of the café when he'd packed up and left and asked to give him a blow job—and maybe more. Angelo just gestured in such a way to hold off the man, shook his head, and walked on. He was still struggling with himself about whether this was something he wanted. He did know, however, that he didn't want it from this tourist. If he wanted it, he wanted it from the brash, arrogant, and superconfident blond American, Brett. And then, perhaps more dangerously, from Doran Kokinos.

Angelo envied Guido in the relationship his interaction with the American in the café had shown—the submissiveness of it, what the submissiveness portended. The meeting of the eyes, the dipping of the head and eyes by the submissive Guido and the raising of his tail. The dominant American covering Guido's body with his, slipping his possessive cock inside Guido, and fucking him into total submission. Guido's sighs at being mastered and taken care of. Angelo couldn't deny that this was what he wanted too.

The next morning when Angelo took the fishing boat out he had intended to go north again. But as he was preparing his boat for launch, he saw that Guido's boat was still in the harbor. This, in itself, was not unusual or a surprise—Guido was not an early riser by preference; by preference he was someone who stumbled down to the harbor in the mid morning with a bad hangover—but it was perplexing to Angelo nonetheless. He was still mulling over the possibilities when it seemed that his boat turned itself south—and then positioned itself off Doran Kokinos's villa.

Angelo purposely didn't look at the beach as he cast his nets off both sides of his boat. But he no longer could pretend to himself that he wasn't interested, and he turned his eyes toward land. He could see a figure on the beach—possibly more than one. He scrambled to find his binoculars and, when he did, lowered himself in the stern of his boat, with only his face peeking over the gunwale, and put the binoculars to his eyes.

It wasn't one; it was two. And they were joined. Guido was standing on a large beach rug, facing the sea and bent over at the waist. The American, Brett, was standing close behind him, with his hands on Guido's hips. Angelo knew what they were doing—but he denied it to himself, reasoning that they may be fucking, but there was no way to be sure.

Almost as if they wanted Angelo to be sure, though, Brett stood back and Guido went down on the blanket, feet facing the sea. Brett knelt between Guido's spread legs, raised and spread them further with hands grabbing the young Italian's ankles, and crouched over him, covering Guido's body with his own, a dominant controlling and possessing a submissive. The coordinated movement of the two left no doubt in Angelo's mind that the American was fucking Guido. The writhing movement of Guido's body clearly told Angelo that Guido was enjoying it—and was getting vigorous attention.

They fucked like long-term lovers, like a submissive bitch being covered, possessed, and bred by a mastiff.

Mouthing a cascade of choice Italian profanity, Angelo pulled his nets back into the boat as quickly as he could—swearing in earnest when he saw that he'd caught some fish that would need to be swept into the hold before he folded the nets.

But as quickly as he could, he had stowed the fish and nets and was chugging his boat back to sea—toward the north, where, he admonished himself, he should have headed to begin with this morning.

* * * *

On the next day Angelo fished to the north, and although it was not his evening to play at the café, he traded with the woman who usually sang that night and did his two sets. The American, Brett, didn't show up. Neither did the Greek shipping magnate, Doran Kokinos, or Guido, for that matter.

The following day, Angelo's boat went south, almost on its own volition, without Angelo willing it to do that. Guido's boat was still in the harbor when he left—as it had been the previous morning and in the afternoon when Angelo returned to Positano. The fishing had been very good, but Angelo hardly noticed that. His mind was completely elsewhere.

That night, when Angelo came from the back of the café to play his second set, the American was sitting at a table well removed from the small platform on which the musicians performed.

One of the waiters, a saucy, flirty little thing named Luciano, who Angelo had always thought was much too flamboyant in manner but who the solitary men tourists of a certain aspect seemed to appreciate, hovered around Brett's table. While Angelo was playing—although he was so tense and frustrated that he hardly knew what he was playing and singing—Brett pulled Luciano down into his lap for a few minutes, and Luciano squealed and pretended to be much flustered. But that little demonstration didn't last for long. All of the time he was manhandling Luciano playfully, the American was staring at Angelo.

After the set was over, Angelo came into the audience and sat down at the American's table.

"You came to the café," Angelo said, knowing it was an idiotic thing to say, but the American didn't seem at all concerned about opening the conversation.

"Yes, I couldn't stay away. And you came to my table."

"The coffee is the best here for coming out at night."

"I wouldn't know. I came for the music. And I came for you."

"I'm afraid I didn't sing and play well tonight," Angelo said. "I was thinking. I've had quite a bit to think about."

"You sang like an angel—as always. I hope you were thinking of me fucking you. That's what I've been thinking of."

"You were thinking of fucking me when you were fucking Guido?" Angelo said, accusingly.

"Yes," Brett answered straight away. "I wanted to fuck you and you didn't let me. I fuck where the opportunities arise."

Angelo looked away. He couldn't look the American in the eye. After a brief pause, he just shrugged.

"Now you want me to fuck you, don't you?" Brett said in a calm, matter-of-fact voice. "You came back to see if I would swim out to you again and you found me fucking your friend, Guido. Now you want me to fuck you on the beach like I was fucking Guido, don't you?"

Angelo just kept looking away and shrugged again. Brett had a hand on his crotch under the surface of the table. Angelo made no attempt to make him move it.

After a long minute, Angelo spoke. "There is a grotto—a cave—down near the water's edge at the rock outcropping marking the northern edge of the property you are staying at. Did you know that?"

"No, I did not. Is that a place you would like to show me?"

"Yes."

"Now?"

"It's nighttime now. It's dark out"

"There are lanterns at the top of the steps down to the beach. My car is not far from here. I have a blanket in the trunk. And here, see, I have condoms in my pocket. What else do we need? And if the lanterns don't work, I can fuck in the dark."

"I have never . . ."

"I can be gentle. I will teach you. You know you want me to fuck you. You must trust me. Do you trust me?"

The American was only gentle at first, but once they were deep into the fuck, Angelo didn't care, and Brett was too intensely

112

into it to care either. Angelo liked it best just as he thought he would—him on all fours and Brett covering his body and fucking him like a dog.

The American stopped his car in the driving court of the villa and they kissed there. They also unzipped each other there and each stroked the other's cock, and Angelo gave no objection when Brett leaned back in the seat and moved Angelo's face to his lap.

"You'd best show me that grotto now," Brett said in a hoarse voice after they'd been sitting in the car for twenty minutes.

"On your hands and knees on the blanket," Brett had said when they'd entered the grotto and he had spread the blanket nearly to the edge of the tidal pool they had had to slither past to get to the rear, sandy-bottomed portion of the cave. He'd put the lantern down on the edge of the pool, and the reflected light on the water of the pool bounced off the uneven ceiling of the cave, sending undulating waves of blue around the small grotto. "You may rest your chest on the blanket, but keep your ass raised. Yes, like that."

He spent some time initially crouched behind Angelo, with an arm wrapped around the young Italian's waist and palming his flat belly, while his other hand snaked between Angelo's thighs and milked his cock and pulled on and fondled his balls. The American's tongue mined Angelo's entrance, loosening and opening it to him. Angelo moaned and groaned at the attention in a volume that increased when Brett moved his mouth from the entrance to swallow Angelo's cock, which had been pulled back between his legs. Angelo's virginal cries of being sucked by a man for the first time reverberated around the small cave.

Angelo came down the American's throat, and started to collapse onto his stomach. But Brett held him in position with the hand palming his belly. The blond gave a low, guttural laugh. "No, this is the right position for your first time. You will be open, and I can fuck you deep. I will take you for a walk on the clouds now. God, you've got a beautiful body. And you taste sweet."

The American rose and covered Angelo's body close from behind in a crouch. Angelo cried out and writhed as the cock slowly entered him. And withdrew a bit and then invaded farther. Out, and in farther.

"Shit. I don't think I can . . ." Angelo pleaded.

"Shush, shush, we're taking it slow. You're so tight. You didn't lie. So tight and so, so sweet."

Angelo whimpered and said that perhaps they should . . . "Oh shit, oh Fuck!" he cried out as Brett began a slow pump. And then faster and deeper. Faster yet. Slap, slap, slap, balls hitting balls. Angelo panting and groaning, his begging for mercy slowly transitioning into begging for more attention.

When Brett tensed and jerked, and came, they held for a moment, the American breathing hard and Angelo's wind hissing between his clinched teeth, his body jerking periodically in a dry sob. Brett slowly turned and rolled to the ground so that he was stretched out on his side and Angelo was cuddled into his chest.

"A few minutes, and then we will make love more than sex," Brett murmured.

Angelo wheezed his fluttering response of being covered, overwhelmed, and totally taken. After a bit, Brett raised Angelo's leg and turned toward him, giving his cock deeper purchase. The staff was hard again.

"Do you want me again?" Brett whispered.

"Yes, oh, yes," Angelo murmured.

Later, when Angelo was almost asleep, Brett pulled himself up—and then Angelo—and he supported Angelo with one arm and carried the lantern with the other as they mounted the steps up to the lower-level terrace.

"I'll just be a minute," the American said. When he came back, he was carrying four frosted bottles of Moretti beer. The two stretched out on patio chairs, naked, and watched the stars in the clear sky.

Half way through the first beer, Brett stood up from his chair and turned to where Angelo was sitting in his chair.

"I want to fuck you again," was all the American said. He reached down and gathered up one of Angelo's legs in each arm and raised and spread them. Angelo threw his head back and watched the stars overhead and moaned, as Brett lifted his buttocks off the chair cushion, split his butt cheeks with a hard cock, and slow fucked him to a second ejaculation for the evening.

114

Angelo clutched Brett's butt cheeks with his hands and groaned and grunted and begged him to fuck deep and to take long strokes. When Brett was done he lowered Angelo's body and returned to his chair and picked up his beer bottle and took another swig.

So, this is how it is, Angelo thought. How simple and natural—and satisfying it was.

Only when they were close to the end of the second beer each did Brett speak again. "You will be in my bed tonight."

"Yes," Angelo answered. No thought to the fishing he should be doing the next day. Just like that all of the priorities of his life had been reordered.

The beers finished, they entered the villa and Angelo followed Brett up a curved staircase of stone treads. This put them in a long hallway. Half way down the corridor, on the sea side of the house, a door was open and a soft light spread out onto the hallway floor. The two silently approached to pass by and Brett put a finger to his lips and gestured toward the open door, indicating that he wanted Angelo to see what was inside.

What was inside was a large bedroom, probably the villa's master bedroom, well appointed in rich furnishings with a definite masculine appearance.

Sitting on the end of the bed, showing to the door to the corridor in side angle, was the Greek tycoon, Doran Kokinos. He was naked. Short and stocky, with coarse features and covered in black curly hair, he looked almost like an evil gnome. But the whole package fit together as more solid than fat, even though he tended to the rotund, and there was no questioning that the man exuded power and charisma. Sitting in his lap, leaving no doubt that his ass was skewered on the Greek's hard phallus, was Guido, facing away from the Greek, the balls of his feet pressed into the thick carpet on the floor.

Angelo involuntarily sucked air when he saw the tableau. It wasn't because he was shocked at seeing Guido being lap fucked by the Greek, although that, indeed, was a surprise. It was because of what was sticking out of Guido's hard, erect cock. The end of a thin steel rod protruded from Guido's piss slit. The Greek was holding the young man's back to his hairy chest with one hand cupping Guido's chin. The Greek's other hand was

115

manipulating the steel rod, revolving it a bit in Guido's piss slit and slowly pushing it in and then pulling it a bit out and then back in, perhaps a little deeper than it had been before. A rolling table had been pulled up on the other side of the pair beside their legs. Angelo could see that there were other, graduated-in-size, steel rods arranged neatly on the table top.

Guido was trembling and whimpering, but he wasn't objecting or trying to get away.

"It's a very delicate procedure," Brett whispered into Angelo's ear from behind. "It's incredibly sensual, but you have to hold perfectly still. The ultimate fuck. Being fucked in two holes at once. The ultimate in sensuality and nirvana for a submissive."

Angelo shuddered. Brett was standing very close behind him, encircling his torso with strong hands. The fingers of one hand thrumming one of Angelo's nipples. "The rods are called wands," the American whispered. "The sex act is called sounding. Have you ever seen—?"

"I've never . . . even . . . . heard of . . ." Angelo answered in a low, stuttering voice that Brett would barely hear and that just sort of wafted into a silence that Angelo couldn't feel.

"When you dipped your eyes to me and the way you surrendered to me when I covered your body," Brett murmured, keeping Angelo encased in his arms. "You are a true submissive, aren't you? You would like to experience the ultimate in submissiveness, wouldn't you?"

Angelo didn't answer, but he gasped when Guido gasped as the steel rod was completely withdrawn from his penis. Then he whimpered as the Greek's fingers picked out one of a larger size—and gasped again as it was being slid into his slit.

"You're hard again," the American whispered in Angelo's ear. "You like what you see. You want it too."

"Noooo," Angelo whined. But he couldn't deny he was hard again—from watching this act that he hadn't, in his wildest dreams—known existed. He felt Brett hard again too, at his back.

He didn't object as the American raised his torso with hands gripping his waist and settled his channel on a hard cock again. Angelo was suspended in front of the American who crouched down a bit to keep them in balance and then began to

116

slowly raise and lower Angelo on his cock as they both looked into the room.

Guido was receiving the fourth graduated wand inside his piss slit, when he began to moan more loudly and to declare that he was close to coming.

Angelo came then himself, shooting out onto the plush carpet of the bedroom. When he looked up at the bed again, Guido was burbling cum around the sides of the buried wand and down onto this thighs. The Greek extracted the last wand and placed it carefully on the tabletop. Then he rose up on his feet, forcing Guido up on his as well, and Guido just bent forward, grabbing at his ankles with his fists. Holding Guido's hips in his hands, the Greek started to pump him from behind.

Angelo was too weak to move and would have collapsed on the floor himself if Brett hadn't been holding him at the waist. The American gathered up the Italian youth in his arms, though, and carried him off to what proved to be his own bed in his own bedroom down the hall.

* * * *

Angelo had been so hyper about how quickly and deeply he had been dropped into male-on-male sex when Brett wanted to go to sleep that the American had suggested that the Italian take a sedative that he offered. This had immediately worked and had kept Angelo so under that when he woke, he discovered he no longer was in Brett's bed but was in a private gym of some sort, with a lot of fancy exercise equipment around. He himself was lying on his back, naked, on some sort of vinyl cube affair and Brett, also naked, was hunched over him, fiddling with some sort of band around his wrist, attaching it to a bound ankle. His ankles already were pulled back toward his waist at the side of the vinyl cube and cuffed to the side of the cube—and his buttocks were raised at the end of the cube.

"What?" Angelo mumbled, still half dazed.

"Do you trust me?" Brett asked. "You must trust me. This is for you. You said to me once that you wanted to leave here. Maybe go to America. We talked about films. Do you want opportunities?"

"Yes, but . . . why am I bound? What are you . . . ?"

Brett was attaching Angelo's second cuffed wrist to the cuff of the ankle already pulled back at one side of the cube.

"You want me to fuck you again don't you?"

"Yes, please. But . . ."

"Lay there and enjoy it as well—and as vocally—as you did in the grotto. We're being watched. You need to trust me."

Brett disappeared from Angelo's sight between his legs, although one of the American's hands remained encircling the Italian's cock and stroking it lightly.

Angelo began to moan as he felt Brett's lips and tongue start to work the rim of his hole.

"Oh, fuck. Oh shit yes. Fuck me," Angelo was mouthing when Brett was crouched over him, his hands working Angelo's nipples and his cock working Angelo's ass. Angelo was moving his hips and raising and lowering them with leverage off the balls of his cuffed feet at the side of the cube to help maximize the still-engaged withdrawal and then the deep plunge of Brett's cock inside him—again and again and again. They were working as one unit despite Angelo being held totally captive by the cuffs.

Angelo was crying out that he was about to come, when Brett stopped and held him close and motionless. "No, you're not," he whispered in Angelo's ear. "Not yet. Stay with me here. This is important to you."

After Angelo's moment of explosion had passed without an ejaculation, Brett raised off him, although still encased in his channel, and reached over and pulled a small, rolling table toward him.

Looking over at that, Angelo's eyes opened wide. "Nooo, pleassse," he pleaded. He began to squirm as violently as his bounds would permit, as Brett held his hard cock firmly and waved a thin sounding wand over the glans.

"You will take this even if we have to give you a sedative again to quiet you down," Brett said in a firm voice. "We are here to please Dodo, and he will get what he wants. If you don't fight it, you will have pleasure as well. If you do fight it, you may be ruined. Do you understand? You must trust me. This will be unbelievably arousing to you. The ultimate fuck. You take this well, and you have a bright future. Are you going to settle down?"

"Please don't. Please let me go."

Brett was holding Angelo's cock firmly and the cold tip of the wand was at Angelo's piss slit, moving around the hole, caressing the rim of the entrance.

"Relax. This needs to go in at the right angle, if you don't want to be ruined. Lay back and enjoy it. But Dodo must know that you will be totally ours. Doors will open to you, but only if you give over total control."

With a sigh of resignation, Angelo collapsed into the vinyl cube. But he was arching his back again, panting heavily, and straining at the cuffs on his ankles and wrists when the American pressed the tip of the wand into the slit opening and then moved it deeper.

"Oh fuck, nooo," Angelo moaned.

"Relax. Breath normally. You'll love it. It's already in. There's nothing to fight anymore."

Angelo panted and moaned, but he did relax back into the cube. He gasped as Brett brought the wand out and then pressed back in. Out and in; out and in.

"Ahhhhhhh."

"Enjoying it now, aren't you?"

Brett released Angelo's cock, leaving the wand buried inside. He laced his fingers through Angelo's balls and distended them. His other hand went to roaming Angelo's chest. "You have such a beautiful body. You deserve to be in films," the American murmured. He began to pump Angelo's channel with his cock.

Ten minutes later, the bulb of Brett's condom filled out inside Angelo, and he pulled out.

Now what? Angelo thought. Does the wand come out?

Now what, was Doran Kokinos appearing from the shadows and taking up the station that Brett had withdrawn from. And, yes, the wand came out. But only to be replaced by a thicker wand. Doran's cock was thicker than Brett's too. Not as long, but quite definitely thicker, and Angelo only having been taken by Brett this far tensed his body, arched his head back, rolled his eyeballs up toward his eyebrows, and whimpered a low and ineffective plea to be released as a thicker cock worked hard to possess his channel and a thicker wand worked its way into Angelo's urethra tube.

119

Kokinos, for all his gnome-like ugliness and coarseness, was a far more masterful cocksman and sounding manipulator than the American was. By closing his eyes and just going with varied rhythms and angles of the Greek's cocking, the working of his free hand on Angelo's body, and the off-beat probing of his piss channel with the thicker wand—and the even thicker one after that—Angelo was lifted to new heights of arousal that he could not deny had him dancing on clouds. He couldn't deny that Brett had been right, that he felt totally taken now as he had not felt with just the ass fucking, as good as it was.

After twice begging for release and being denied, Kokinos let Angelo come during the fourth stage of the wands. The Greek had not come, however.

He called Brett over and told him he could release Angelo. "You may have him for the day. Teach him the positions you know I like. He will do very nicely. He will be in my bed tonight."

Brett released an exhausted Angelo, slung him over his shoulder, and took him out of the exercise room en route to his bedroom. As they were leaving, Angelo lifted his eyes from the floor and caught a glimpse of Kokinos, his thick cock still hard and curved up, approaching another apparatus. Angelo saw Guido, his legs raised and spread wide, cuffed at the ankles on a frame. He was naked, on his back, and his cock was standing straight up—with two wands protruding from the piss slit. Angelo heard the other young Italian fisherman cry out, as the Greek moved between his legs, thrust his hips forward and up, and began to pump.

That night, although smaller than Angelo, the Greek was solid muscle and much more powerful than the young Italian. He slung the younger man around in countless positions—more than Brett had shown Angelo over the afternoon—and showed over and over again throughout the night that he could come again and again—and could make Angelo do so as well.

At first Angelo was disconcerted by the flashes going off around the bed in a constant rhythm, but he grew used to it—just as he increasingly became addicted to the Greek tycoon's expert fucking. By dawn, when the Greek told him that Brett would drive him back to his boat in the Positano harbor, Angelo didn't want anything as much as the Greek's cock inside him, working its magic.

* * * *

Brett dropped Angelo off in the Positano harbor late the next morning, and Angelo hobbled home rather than to his boat, almost not being able to mount the steep-sloped cobblestoned street to his building because of the glorious soreness in his channel and the aching of the leg muscles he'd used to keep his legs spread during the previous day and night, muscles he didn't normally use in his fishing—certainly not in any way like this.

Before he went up into the town, however, he checked Guido's fishing boat. It was still in the harbor, and Guido wasn't in it.

Angelo slept most of the day, only managing to get up in time to make his set at the café. Neither the Greek nor the American nor Guido showed up at the café. Only the flirty Luciano fluttering around, teasing a couple of middle-aged male tourists existed at the café to remind Angelo of the lifestyle that he had fallen into. He surprised himself by thinking of the Greek and his cock—and the sounding—more than he did about the American. So, it wasn't the beauty of a well-toned, young body that was attracting him. It was the mystery of the sounding and, above all, the mastery of a cock wielded by an experienced lover. And it was like Brett had told to him. His greatest arousal was in being totally controlled, totally possessed. And the sounding wand—in addition to being bound immobile and having a cock inside his ass canal—was the ultimate submissive sensation.

The next day, Angelo took his fishing boat out. He had to. He had to put food on his table. He went north rather than south, willing himself to do necessary work.

When Brett had left him off in the harbor, he said that he would come for Angelo when the Greek wanted him. Angelo assumed that would be the next day, but it wasn't. And it wasn't the next day either. On the afternoon of the second day, on which Angelo took the fishing boat south, to the fishing ground off Kokinos's villa to spend more of the day with his binoculars than with his net, he did not see any activity at the villa. Angelo checked out Guido's boat again. It still hadn't left the harbor.

And this time Guido's boat had a "For Sale" sign on it.

"What do you know about Guido?" Angelo asked when he stopped at the fish market by the pier where Guido's boat was lashed up. "His boat has a 'For Sale' sign on it."

"I don't know. I haven't seen Guido in days. But I've heard that he already has left Positano."

"Left Positano?" Angelo was bewildered.

"Some say he has gone to Cyprus."

"To Cyprus? What's in Cyprus?"

"Well, his lawyer—who is trying to sell the boat—says that Guido is going to be in movies."

"In movies? Movies are filmed in Cyprus?"

"One supposes, but I don't know. I just know that Guido's family has had that boat for generations, and I think he must be crazy to be selling it and leaving our little slice of heaven. They say he's gone to Limassol, which is on Cyprus' south coast."

Angelo gave the man a dull look. Could he be serious, or was he poking fun? Not want to leave Positano? It had been Angelo's dream for years to leave Positano—and even to be in movies. And now Guido was already doing it? Before him or rather than him?

Even though it was late in the afternoon and it would be dark before he returned, Angelo climbed the hill to his home, took his motorbike out of the shed in the garden at the back, and drove the coastal road south.

No one answered at the gates of the Kokinos villa and, although Angelo found a place that he could scale the wall and get into the compound, there was no sign that anyone was there.

Forlorn, Angelo puttered back to Positano and, over the next three weeks, did what he could to return his life to normal. Of course he no longer could return to what he had known as normal before he found man-to-man sex and the ultimate submissive act. Guido's lawyer had been making oblique suggestions to him for a couple of years. He was in his late forties and not bad looking, and he kept himself in trim condition. He had, in fact, been a bone of contention between Angelo and Guido. Guido had been willing to lay under the man, but the

122

lawyer had made clear that he preferred Angelo. And yet Angelo had pretended that there was nothing on offer that he was interested in.

Angelo now surprised the man, though. He came to his door on a Saturday afternoon when Angelo knew that the lawyer's wife and their housekeeper were in Salerno buying goods they couldn't find in Positano. Angelo had taken him by the hand and led him to the man's bed and let the lawyer fuck him. Over the weeks, the lawyer had regularly been appearing at the café in the evening and had gone to Angelo's rooms and fucked him and then gone home to his wife. It was something, but not really enough for Angelo. The man did not have the imagination nor the demanding nature of either the American, Brett, or the Greek, Doran Kokinos. And he knew nothing about sounding. Angelo didn't even know where he could buy a sounding kit.

But what the lawyer provided was something, better than nothing. And the lawyer was totally smitten with his good luck.

* * * *

"Strip. This man is going to fuck you. And if he likes you, he will make you a film star."

"A film star?" Angelo asked.

"Yes, he is a film director. From Cyprus. He makes men's art films," Doran Kokinos answered. "Limassol is one of the gay male sex film capitals of the world. He can take you to Cyprus and put you into films."

Angelo's mind ran to Guido, who had not returned to Positano. The mention of films and Cyprus had told Angelo that this, no doubt, had been where Guido had gone. He also now clearly understood what was happening here. It wasn't just the man—another tall Greek, hefty but not fat, with wavy black hair on his head, and black hair curling around and down his chest too—although not as much as Kokinos had—and a face that only a mother could love, but arousing in a thuggish way—and Kokinos and Angelo in the exercise room in Kokinos's villa. Off to the side, the fluttery waiter from the café, Luciano, was cuffed to the vinyl cube, and Brett was fucking him and introducing him to the sounding wands. The little slut was bawling like a baby, but

123

he wasn't convincing. He was loving the attention and every other man in the room knew it.

The film director walked around Angelo when he was stripped, gliding his hand over this, gently prodding that. He laced his hands through Angelo's balls and brought the young Italian close in to his body. They kissed and then the director went down on his knees before Angelo and gave him a blow job that was expert and had Angelo panting hard and ejaculating when the director told him he was free to do so.

Then it was Angelo's turn to go on his knees and open his mouth. Brett and Doran had already taught him how to do this, and Angelo clearly understood that they had been testing and training him three weeks earlier. They had been recruiting here. No doubt they recruited elsewhere as well.

"Down on all fours," the director commanded before he had come. Angelo went down on an exercise mat. Brett came over to join them. Doran had taken over at the cube, and had a thicker cock inside Luciano and a thicker wand in the young man's penis. His penis was small, but most of the wand had disappeared inside him regardless. Luciano was quiet now, his head lolled over to the side, a trapped expression on his face.

Brett went down between Angelo's legs. A hand encased Angelo's cock, and Brett's tongue and lips went to his rear entrance. The director stood in front of Angelo, feeding his cock into Angelo's mouth.

When Angelo's channel was ready, the director took him in multiple positions, Angelo being taken through the paces of the positions that he now realized that Brett and Doran had been teaching to him just for this very moment. Angelo wondered what their finders' fees would be. But he found that he didn't care anymore, not really.

The director was both thicker than Doran and longer than Brett, and he fucked Angelo without mercy, suggesting—even though no offer had been voiced as yet—that he needed to know what Angelo's limits were, if any. Angelo almost reached those limits when the director laid on his back on the mat, brought Angelo down on his cock, pulled Angelo's torso back to where he was lying on the man's chest, and then Brett knelt between their legs and fed his cock into Angelo as well and started pumping.

When they finished, the director pushed Angelo off his body and disappeared for a few minutes. Brett was still crouched next to Angelo.

"Is that all?" Angelo whispered.

"He specializes in movies with sounding in them," Brett murmured back. "You must trust us. You wanted to get out of Positano and even wanted to be in movies. You trust me, don't you?"

Trust you? Angelo thought. I don't trust you as far as I can throw you.

But then the director was back and Angelo was being lifted and laid on his back on the apparatus he'd last seen Guido on. His legs were being raised and spread and cuffed on a frame. And Brett was rolling the table with the sounding wands on them over to the apparatus. Doran had already released Luciano from the cube and carried him away, no doubt to his bed for further conditioning. The director picked up a thick wand—a thicker one than Angelo could remember having been used on him before. He moved between Angelo's legs and Angelo gasped and arched his back as a long, thick cock slid up into his channel. The man smiled a wicked smile and lifted the wand.

Angelo set his jaw, trying not to cry out, although the director had told him that he could—that it was something that would be good in the films. It was the best opportunity he was likely to get to come anywhere close to achieving his goals. Yes, he would tell these men he trusted them, if that's what it took to be a movie star and to have someone who would give him full sexual satisfaction.

About the Author

Habu is one of the pen names of a former supersonic spy jet pilot, intelligence agent, male model, movie actor, and diplomat. A wild youth in South East Asia was spent enjoying whatever sexual opportunities came his way, and much of his gay male writing is about recalling incidents from those days and inventing ones he'd perhaps have liked to experience. He now leads a very quiet and ordinary happily married family life.

An American, he is a published mainstream novelist and short story writer under another name and in another dimension of his life. He has written or cowritten (with Sabb) over 500 published short stories and nearly 100 published erotica e-books, primarily of gay fiction but also memoir, straight fiction and ménage fiction. His hand and creative writing can be seen in stories and books by habu, sr71plt, Dirk Hessian, Shabbu, and Stephen Kessel—among unrevealed others that might surprise readers. The fictionalized GM memoir *Flying High, Diving Deep* is loosely based on his life experiences. He can be found at the adults only gay male site www.BarbarianSpy.com, which he shares with Sabb and Dirk Hessian.

Our authors always like to receive feedback, and appreciate it when readers post reviews at Goodreads, and other sites.

BarbarianSpy
FOR LITERARY HEAT

Not all books listed below may currently be on release.
BOOKS BY DIRK HESSIAN
Xtreme Erotica
The King's Men
Shores of Tripoli
Prophecy of Noto
Pretender's Fate
General Erotica/Romance
Constantinople
The Beautiful Way
Blue and Gray
Colonel's Treasure
Beginning of Time
Labyrinth
BOOKS BY HABU
Gay Erotica
Memoir Faction
Flying High, Diving Deep*
Xtreme Erotica
Second Coming
Vortex: Sacrificed by Curiosity*
Dark Angel Sounding *(included in Sounding:Ultimate Control)**
Sounding: Ultimate Control (Print Only)*
Sounding Five (E-book only)
General Erotica
Romance
Lower Than the Heart
Brambleton
Gotta Keep Trying
Finding Amnad
Platres Conclave
Other
Dance of the Ravishers
Beyond the Beaded Curtain*
Hard Knocks U*
Habu's Christmas Balls

My Neighbor's Spa
Man's Man*
Trip Money
Clint Folsom Mysteries Compendium Volume 1*
Death to Blonds - Stolen Judgment (Clint Folsom Mystery)
Clint Folsom Mysteries Compendium Volume 2*
Grab Bag 1*
Grab Bag 2*
Grab Bag 3*
The Indian Doctor
Sailorboy
Home to Fire Island
The Sporting Life*
Fetish Galore!*
Choke Hold
Literary Gay Erotica
Cairo Surrender*
The Handyman*
Homeward Bound
Journey to Mirage*
Menage Erotica
13 Ways for Halloween
Luther*
The Indian Prince
BOOKS BY SHABBU
Finding Jason
Dirty Pool
Operation Black Jade
Cigars!*
Angel in the Barn
Gayly Complicated
Despoiling David
The Tree of Idleness
I Met a Man
The Interview
Rough Road to Happiness
BOOKS BY SABB
Hiring in Hollywood
The Legend of Holleystone Grange
Surprise Encounters
She is He

Wrong Man
Loyal to his King
Barbarian Tales - Book One - Traveler's Tales*
Barbarian Tales - Book Two - Journeys Begin*
Barbarian Tales - Book Three - The Inheritance*
Barbarian Tales - Book Four - Road to Persepolis*
~
* indicates the book is available in paperback and e-book.